JORY STRONG

BINDING
FALLON MATES
KRISTA

ELLORA'S CAVE
ROMANTICA PUBLISHING

What the critics are saying...

∞

"Jory Strong has a wonderful and colorful imagination. It is always difficult creating a new world for science fiction stories." ~ *The Romance Readers Connection*

"Fallon Mates: Binding Krista is a wonderful tale about the love that is found by three people. It would seem that finding such a love is impossible but Jory Strong has created a story and people who will make readers think that maybe it's not as impossible as it seems. I greatly enjoyed reading Binding Krista and look forward to more of Jory Strong's work and more of her Fallon Mate series." ~ *A Romance Review*

"Binding Krista was a great beginning and sets the standard for the upcoming books. It was an extremely wild and fun ride through the future with lots of action on every level with three entrancing characters." ~ *Love Romances*

An Ellora's Cave Romantica Publication

www.ellorascave.com

Content Advisory:

S – ENSUOUS
E – ROTIC
X – TREME

Ellora's Cave Publishing offers three levels of Romantica™ reading entertainment: S (S-ensuous), E (E-rotic), and X (X-treme).

The following material contains graphic sexual content meant for mature readers. This story has been rated E–rotic.

S-*ensuous* love scenes are explicit and leave nothing to the imagination.

E-*rotic* love scenes are explicit, leave nothing to the imagination, and are high in volume per the overall word count. E-rated titles might contain material that some readers find objectionable—in other words, almost anything goes, sexually. E-rated titles are the most graphic titles we carry in terms of both sexual language and descriptiveness in these works of literature.

X-*treme* titles differ from E-rated titles only in plot premise and storyline execution. Stories designated with the letter X tend to contain difficult or controversial subject matter not for the faint of heart.

Also by Jory Strong

About the Author

❧

Jory has been writing since childhood and has never outgrown being a daydreamer. When she's not hunched over her computer, lost in the muse and conjuring up new heroes and heroines, she can usually be found reading, riding her horses, or hiking with her dogs.

Jory welcomes comments from readers. You can find her website and email address on her author bio page at www.ellorascave.com.

Tell Us What You Think

We appreciate hearing reader opinions about our books. You can email us at Comments@EllorasCave.com.

BINDING KRISTA

∽

Dedication

❧

No writer succeeds without having both a good editor and a good publishing house behind them. I'm fortunate enough to have both.

My thanks to Sue-Ellen Gower, whose suggestions have made my manuscripts richer and fuller for passing through her hands, and whose praise and encouragement challenge me to make each story better than the previous one.

My thanks also to all those both behind the scenes and in the forefront who have made and continue to make Ellora's Cave the premier publisher of women's romantica.

Trademarks Acknowledgement

❧

The author acknowledges the trademarked status and trademark owners of the following wordmarks mentioned in this work of fiction:

Advil: Boots Company PLC

Beemer (BMW): Bayerische Motoren Werke Aktiengesellschaft

Chapter One

ℬ

Adan d'Amato grimaced as he studied the scene in front of him. Gambler's Paradise they called this place, but it was more likely Gambler's Hell.

Humans were packed in like miners on an old Ewellian transport. Between the noise that their mechanical machines made, and the sound of their voices, it was enough to send a less-seasoned warrior running for cover.

At Adan's side, Lyan d'Vesti wore a fierce scowl. His mood was echoed in his mind-thought. *The Council wastes our time. We'll find no bond-mate here.*

Adan laughed softly at Lyan's impatience. *Our mate will arrive. Whoever watches over her would not send us to this location if she were not going to be here.*

Lyan snorted. *You have too much respect for the infallibility of the Council and its genetic scientists. Their predictions and equations do not always hold true in the real world. Have I not told them so each time I was hauled before them to explain my actions? It would amuse them to send us on a wild chase, or mate us to a human with nothing of the Fallon in her. But if this human mate is unsuitable, then I will have one of my own choosing. The Vesti take what belongs to them when the time is right to take it. We do not beg at the table of the Council.*

Adan didn't bother hiding the amusement in his thoughts. *No doubt you have managed to offend someone on the Council, if not all of the members. But I have been a model citizen. When the marker in your genes was matched to the human's, the scientists had to know that you would choose me to complete the mate-bond. No doubt they would have welcomed the extinction of your traits, but because of the respect they hold for mine, they told you of the woman's existence.*

Lyan shifted impatiently. *We will see if you remain amused as this plays out.*

In front of the warriors, a red light suddenly began flashing. A siren screamed and an elderly human female with blue-tinted hair squealed in a tone pitched high enough to shatter Sarien glass. Only reflexes honed by hours of training and years of experience kept Adan and Lyan from using the Ylan crystals on their wrists to transmute the offending machine into particles so small that it could never be recovered.

Coins began tumbling out of the machine the elderly human had been hovering over. Lyan shook his head in amazement. *Coins! It has been thousands of years since our ancestors were here and yet these humans continue to evolve at the creeping pace of a Tresor slug. No wonder our appearance gave rise to their legends of angels and demons!*

Adan shrugged. *Be glad that some of the Fallon were drawn to these humans and bred with them. If not for the genes of our shared ancestors, there would be no hope for either the Vesti or the Amato and both of our races would be doomed to extinction.*

Lyan fought down the fury that always threatened to consume him at the mention of the fate awaiting those on Belizair. His heart raged at the pain his elder brother and his brother's mate endured. Unless the genetic scientists found a solution to the bio-gene virus the Hotalings had let loose on Belizair, his brother's pairing would produce no children. Nor would there be children for any of the Amato or Vesti females.

So far the scientists had found only one way to defeat the Hotaling virus. Now the Council's agents searched among the humans in order to identify those females who had the genetic marker of one of the Fallon—the shared ancestor race of the Amato and Vesti.

All hope to avoid extinction rested on the unmated males, yet each male carried both the fear that there would be no match and the knowledge that it required a Vesti or Amato co-mate in order to produce offspring.

Lyan forced the tightness out of his chest. He was the first of his family to be matched. The continuance of their line rested with him—and Adan. He had never been drawn to females outside of his race but... Even as the thought took form, a woman entered the casino and need shot through his cock.

Suddenly he had to fight for air, fight even to keep his balance. The purple-colored Ylan crystals woven into the wristbands bearing the symbol of Lyan's clan-house burned against his skin, echoing the searing heat swirling through his very bloodstream.

Adan took a sharp intake of breath, his eyes zeroing in on the woman. The deep gold Ylan crystals on his wrists swirled as his emotions surged in recognition of their mate's presence. "By the Council, she is exquisite," Adan murmured as he placed a hand on Lyan's shoulder.

Lyan's nostrils flared as every predatory instinct within him focused on their mate. She was small, even among her own people, and dressed in black—the color of a warrior's clothing. And yet her body was made for pleasure, not fighting.

Against the black material, her hair was a golden torch. Lyan could imagine the silky heat of it burning its way across his skin and inflaming him further as it flowed over their writhing bodies. The mating fever of the Vesti race shimmered just below the surface of his control. His cock was fully engorged, rock-hard, ready. Instinct urged him to pounce now, to take her, join with her, make her completely his. A low growl vibrated along his throat.

Like a cool wind, Adan's voice whispered, warned. *And to take her that way is to guarantee there will be no offspring for either of us. It is not one or the other, it is both or there is no conception at all.*

The growl in Lyan's throat deepened. He snarled. *Curse the Hotalings and their get. Let our people hunt them down one by one and rid the universe of them for their use of the bio-gene weapons.*

And we will. But for now let us be glad that our scientists have found a way for us to avoid extinction. Our mate awaits. Do we stand here and argue what cannot be changed, or do we go and secure her so that through her womb our lines may both survive?

Adan didn't wait for an answer, but stepped forward. As he did so, the woman sensed his movement and looked at him. He was too skilled a hunter not to see her tense, ready herself to escape. Her reaction flooded his being with the desire to protect her even as blood pounded through his shaft in anticipation of a chase. Let her run. The victory and mating would only be that much more intense. On his wristbands, the gold crystals swirled in tune to his anticipation of a mate, an heir, the survival of his race.

Lyan's voice growled in his mind. *Now whose lust threatens to leave us without a mate? She must accept us willingly or there is no bond.*

Adan laughed softly. *Do you really doubt our ability to secure our bond-mate? Before this night is over, she will belong to us in all ways.*

* * * * *

Krista Thomas felt their gaze as soon as she entered the casino. She'd been on the run for so long that her first instinct was to bolt. But as she surreptitiously studied the two men, she hesitated. They were dangerous, there was no doubt about that, but were they dangerous to her?

She laughed silently, for a split second allowing some of the ever-present tension to drop from her shoulders. They were certainly dangerous to her libido. God, they were a walking fantasy.

Even in Las Vegas, a sin city where beauty and wealth flashed twenty-four/seven, those two turned heads. Gorgeous didn't do them justice. They were stunning, with their fierce, confident warrior bodies and ultra-masculine faces. Krista wanted to press against them, run her hands through their silky shoulder-length hair—one golden blond, the other raven black.

She took a deep breath instead.

Fantasy was a luxury she couldn't afford.

True, the men in question didn't look like the type of men Alexi would hire, in fact they were the complete opposite. But she couldn't afford to drop her guard.

If Alexi caught her…

An involuntary shiver raced along Krista's spine. Lately the men she'd eluded had looked as though they would be willing to bring her in dead or alive.

Soon she'd have to call the DA and see if there was a court date. It was risky making contact, but she needed to know if Alexi had reason to put out a contract on her.

Another shiver ripped through her. She couldn't let herself think about it, not now. Now she had to concentrate on winning enough money to stay on the run. If she was lucky, she could stay in Las Vegas a few more days before she was spotted. Being here at all was a calculated risk, especially after Atlantic City, but gambling was the only way—or at least the only acceptable way—of getting the money she needed to survive. She took a deep breath and moved toward a line of slot machines close to the blackjack tables.

The blackjack dealers were doing a booming business. From the looks of it, there was some kind of sales convention in town. Krista shook her head slightly and silently laughed at herself. This was Vegas, of course there was a convention here. Wasn't there always?

She ran her fingers over the tokens in her pocket. Her stomach gave a low rumble and spasmed, reminding her of the pressing need to eat. The last real meal had been days ago, just before she bolted from Los Angeles. The last time she'd actually relaxed in a restaurant and savored her food seemed like a lifetime ago.

Krista glanced around, still hyperaware of her surroundings, especially of the two men watching her. She stopped in front of the first slot machine and slipped a coin in, only vaguely aware of the results as she covertly monitored the two men. The blond man moved in her direction. The other stepped forward immediately.

Stay or run? Stay or run? The question flashed in her mind as her survival instincts raced to evaluate the situation. She tensed, heart pounding.

The raven-haired man lightly touched his companion's arm. They slowed.

Krista eased back toward the doorway, waiting to see if they'd split and try to trap her between them. There was no doubt that she was their destination. It was in their eyes, in the hard focus of their bodies.

The blond smiled, a surprisingly gentle smile for a man who looked as though there was no softness in him. Krista hesitated again. The stakes were so high. If she was wrong about the men, she'd pay a terrible price—her freedom at a minimum, her life eventually. But something urged that she let them approach and so she stood her ground.

Krista didn't know whether it was anticipation or trepidation that had her heart thundering in her ears and her nerves tingling as the two men came to a stop in front of her. They were so large that she felt surrounded by them even though they'd allowed her an escape route by not getting between her and the door.

"I am Adan d'Amato," the blond said, offering his hand.

Krista placed her hand in his, momentarily transfixed by the wide silver wristband he was wearing. It was ornately carved with huge beasts that resembled saber-toothed cats, but what held her attention was the deep gold crystal in its center.

She'd never seen anything like it. In the casino lighting the gem seemed to swirl and change, almost as if it was alive.

A second hand moved into her line of vision, drawing her eyes away from the gold crystal. "I am Lyan d'Vesti," the dark-haired man said. He, too, wore elaborately carved wristbands, though the purple crystals at his wrists were set among dragons maybe...or some type of winged creatures.

Krista gently tried to pull her hand from Adan's grip, but he held it firmly, and before she could tell him to release it, Lyan reached for her other hand. As soon as his skin touched hers, intense pleasure charged through Krista's arms like an erotic surge of electricity. Her nipples tightened into hard, needy points while a different type of hunger ripped through her abdomen and made her clit throb and the lips of her labia swell. She gasped involuntarily and even as her face flushed with a combination of embarrassment and lust, she raised it to look into Adan and Lyan's faces.

They wore identical expressions—of satisfaction and expectation...of possession.

* * * * *

By the Council, she is ours! Adan's voice penetrated the red haze of desire that had completely filled Lyan's mind at the first touch of their mate.

Let us get her out of here. My cock threatens to rip through this primitive garb! Lyan sent back.

As does mine. But even now she begins to panic. We must soothe and gentle her, Adan said as he brought their mate's hand to his lips and gently pressed a kiss into her palm. Her eyes widened and darkened as a small shiver passed through her. "And you are?" he asked.

"Krista."

"Krista." Adan breathed. Tasting the name. Feeling it on his tongue. It was right. "We have just arrived in your city. Would you care to join us for a meal?"

Lyan's voice growled in his mind. *I would spread her out before me and taste every inch of her skin. I would feast on the desire that belongs to no other from this moment forward.*

Adan chuckled. *For a great Vesti hunter, you lack patience, my friend.*

Do not goad me. Even now I fight against my own nature.

Curse the Hotalings and their weapons! Were it not for them, he would simply take what he wanted. There would be no sharing of his mate, even with one such as Adan, a friend he would die for!

It was not the way of the Vesti to share. They were not the Amato who bonded in whatever variation was agreeable to those involved. The Vesti took one mate and possessed her completely, totally, thoroughly—in every way that a male can claim his female.

Lyan took a deep breath and forced his thoughts in another direction. What was done was done. This was no action hastily entered, only to be regretted later. He loved Adan like a brother. There was no other that he could stand to see covering his…*their* mate, pumping into her as she screamed her pleasure.

His jaws clenched against the need to nuzzle his lips in the tender spot at the base of Krista's neck, to let his mating teeth finally slip out of their hidden sheaths and sink into her body, marking her, making it impossible for her to elude him. He growled into Adan's mind. *Let us get on with it!*

Adan's chuckle rubbed like sandpaper against Lyan's lust-abraded nerves. *While you were busy fantasizing about our mate, I was busy getting her to agree to dine with us. Are you ready to join the conversation now…before she determines that you are in fact the beast you were named for?*

Lyan growled in response but he released Krista's hand and slid his fingers upward so that he could cup her elbow as they moved through the crowded casino.

Chapter Two

ဢ

Krista shivered as she allowed Adan and Lyan to seat her in the casino's Mexican-style restaurant. They'd chosen a quiet, out-of-the-way corner.

As soon as the waiter left to get their drinks, Krista disappeared behind her open menu, grabbing the chance to relax for a moment. Though she couldn't see Adan and Lyan, she could feel the heat pouring off their bodies as they sat on either side of her, containing her, and yet making her feel protected as well. It was the first time in months that she'd felt safe.

Better not get used to it, the voice of reason whispered along her spine. *Fear is what's kept you alive.*

Her hand trembled slightly. Emotional exhaustion and despair threatened to swamp her. She took a deep breath and pushed the destructive feelings away. She needed some downtime. If she stayed this strung out she'd end up dead.

Fingers lightly stroked her shoulder and she startled, ready to jump from her seat until Adan's smooth voice calmed her, "Are you ready to order? Lyan and I thought to try the fajitas. Would you care to share our choice?"

Krista lowered the menu. She'd been so caught in her own turmoil that she hadn't looked at it, much less given any thought to what she wanted to eat. Her strawberry daiquiri sat in front of her, the waiter now hovered, ready to take their order and move on to another customer. She closed the menu and handed it to him with a smile. "Fajitas are fine."

Once again the waiter disappeared, only this time she had nothing to hide her thoughts behind. Krista took a deep breath to center herself as she studied the two men who shared her table.

They were straight out of an erotic fantasy. Unparalleled pleasure and dark desire. She wanted to melt into them, surround herself with their strength.

Adan reached over and covered her hand with his. The rough heat of him contrasted sharply with the cold smoothness of the wooden table. "Tell us about yourself," he urged.

Just his voice sent desire racing along her nerve endings, tightening her nipples and making her cunt wet, readying her for him. With a small intake of breath, she tried to steady herself. She couldn't afford to involve anyone else in her life right now.

Reluctantly she pulled her hand out from underneath Adan's. "There's not much to tell," she said as she shifted her focus to Lyan, hoping that by doing so she could distract herself, lessen the ache between her thighs.

It didn't work.

Lyan's face was slightly flushed. His coal black eyes were focused on her with hungry intent. He was all predator, a male whose very nature would demand submission. Krista knew that it should scare her, not excite and tempt her.

She hastily turned her attention to the daiquiri in front of her and reached for it, only barely able to keep her hand from shaking. The cool drink slid down her throat.

What was she going to do about this—about them?

Why not let nature take its course? the voice of lust whispered in her mind.

And end up sleeping with both of them?

Erotic images flashed through Krista's mind. It was a favorite fantasy of hers—though Adan and Lyan were better in the flesh than any of the partners she'd ever dreamed up.

She resolutely pushed the thoughts away. It was one thing to fantasize, another to actually be with two men at once.

Once again Adan's fingers stroked along her shoulder. "Come, tell us a little something about yourself. What kind of work do you do?"

Krista smiled despite the wave of sadness that washed over her. When this was all over...if she survived...maybe she'd get to do what she loved again. "I'm a teacher."

Adan grinned. "Perhaps I will sign up for one of your classes." He took her hand in his and brought it to his lips, pressing a soft kiss on the palm. "Tell me what I would learn."

"I'm not sure I could teach you anything new." Her voice sounded husky even to her own ears. She felt him smile against her palm, saw it in the crinkle of his eyes. He pressed another kiss into her palm and stroked the soft skin covering her hand. Every touch heightened her awareness of him. To distract herself, she said, "I teach high-school math."

Adan's eyes darkened. "So you like children."

"Yes. Very much."

"But you do not have any of your own."

"No, not yet. What about you?"

Adan smiled. "No. I have not sought a bond-mate until now."

"A bond-mate?"

Adan hesitated. "A shared-wife. A mate to have children with."

Krista closed her eyes briefly, heated by the erotic fantasy he was weaving, by the illusion he was fashioning. Her soul craved the world that he was creating with his words and wanted to take sanctuary in it, to make it her reality. She was so wet that she could smell her own arousal and wondered if they could, too.

A low growl from Lyan drew Krista's attention to him. His eyes were fixed on her chest, on the clear outline of her nipples. His desire was blatant, there for anyone to see, and Krista knew that if she'd allow it, he'd lean across the table and suckle the engorged tips of her breasts right then and there.

She licked her lips nervously and watched Lyan's face tighten. The surge of feminine power that engulfed Krista was as thrilling as it was unfamiliar. In that moment she wanted to lead them to a bedroom and experience her fantasy.

Adan slowly traced his tongue along the lifeline crossing her palm. "How is it that you are unclaimed?"

She pushed her fantasy aside and said, "I've been traveling a lot lately. It doesn't leave any room for getting involved." She knew it was the perfect moment to set limits, to tell them that she wasn't available even for a one-night stand, that they shouldn't be sitting with her now, but she couldn't bring herself to do it. Their heat and desire drew her to them as surely as a moth was drawn to a flame.

Adan's eyebrows rose in question. "You travel with your students?"

"No. I'm between teaching jobs right now."

"You live here in Las Vegas?" Adan asked.

Krista shook her head. "Just visiting. What about you two?"

The two men exchanged a glance and some of Krista's wariness returned. As if sensing her suspicion, Adan smiled and said, "Like you, we are also traveling."

His answer felt like an evasion, but Krista decided not to press him further. What would be the point? This moment in time was a burst of light and fantasy, something to be savored as she evaded the darkness of Alexi's grasp and tried to stay alive.

The chill of reality returned and she slowly pulled her hand out of Adan's grasp. It would be unfair to draw them into her world. She couldn't know what price they might have to pay.

The waiter arrived with a sizzling platter of food. Krista's stomach growled and her mouth watered as she reached for a tortilla and began creating a fajita. For quite a while afterward she could do nothing but concentrate on her meal. It had been so long since she'd done more than grab her food and keep moving. When she was finally full, she let the waiter collect her plate.

Adan had yet to finish eating so Krista shifted her attention to Lyan—the quiet one. "How long will you be here in Vegas?" she asked.

"Only as long as we have to be."

Krista laughed at the cryptic answer. "You don't like to gamble?"

Lyan's eyes flared as he leaned closer. "The outcome is not in doubt. We will leave with what we came for."

Shivers danced up Krista's spine, urging her to close the gap and press her lips to his even as some internal alarm signaled that she should bolt. In desperation, she tried to get control of her warring emotions by reverting to polite conversation.

"What kind of work do you do?"

There was a brief pause as Lyan glanced at Adan, then returned his gaze to Krista. "We are bounty hunters."

White noise filled her mind and for a second Krista thought she was going to faint. Only sheer force of will prevented her from escaping into that welcoming oblivion.

Fear made it almost unbearable to breathe. She'd known since New York that Alexi had started using men who weren't members of his organization to try and locate her.

Adan's fingers gently stroked across her shoulder, only there was no pleasure in his touch this time. "It is not as terrible as it seems," he murmured.

She wanted to laugh hysterically. Instead she fought to gather her wits. The waiter reappeared and asked if they'd like dessert. Krista forced herself to smile and order flan, then as the waiter offered suggestions to Adan, she quickly excused herself and headed toward the sign marking the restrooms. As soon as she rounded the corner, she escaped from the restaurant and bolted out of the casino.

*   *   *   *   *

"I do not like this," Lyan said as he stared at the dessert that sat untouched at Krista's place. *Surely our mate does not think so much is lacking in her appearance that she needs to beautify herself for such a long period of time.*

"I do not like it either," Adan agreed with a frown. He pushed himself away from the table. "I will find someone to check the bathroom."

Lyan nodded in agreement and watched as Adan stalked across the restaurant. Within seconds the waiter came to the table, perhaps sensing that all was not well and wanting to ensure that the dinner was paid for before the situation deteriorated. Lyan took the bill and quickly paid it, making sure to give a generous tip. It was a little thing to him, a habit developed over many years. Generous tips often eased the flow of information, if not today, then sometime in the future. He frowned at the thought. Once their mate was secured, he hoped that he wouldn't have to return to this primitive planet.

Adan's face was stormy as he came back into sight. Lyan knew without words passing between them that their mate was gone. *Was she taken?*

No. She was seen hurrying from the restaurant.

There was pain in Adan's words, a pain that echoed in Lyan's chest. *We will find her.*

Adan nodded. *And when we do, you will mark her in the way of your people so that she cannot elude us again.*

Agreed.

Chapter Three

ஐ

When Krista's panic subsided, the voice of reason reasserted itself and she felt guilty for running out on Adan and Lyan. They might be bounty hunters, but they weren't after her. They couldn't be.

Her entire feminine being screamed that they'd been seeking their own pleasure, had intended to seduce her, not hand her over to another man. They wouldn't have dared to touch her if that was their intent. Even if they didn't know the true reason she was being hunted, they would have known about Alexi's obsession, would have been warned that anything other than catching her and bringing her to him would mean their deaths.

Krista wanted to crawl under warm covers and pretend this was all a nightmare. But she couldn't.

A man had been murdered right in front of her eyes.

Not just any man, but a policeman.

Her heart lurched at the memory.

She grieved for the man and for his family, his wife and small daughter, even though she'd never met any of them. Hadn't even known that he was an undercover agent until months later—after she'd escaped from Alexi and seen an article in the newspaper detailing how the policeman's body had washed up on a beach and been found by tourists.

Even now the scene in the pool house unfolded in her dreams and in the moments when her mind dropped its guard.

If only she'd stayed in the dining room as Alexi had told her to do…

But then she wouldn't have witnessed the murder, wouldn't have known what Alexi was until after she'd married him.

She had to stay alive, had to bear witness for the man who had lost his life, to see that justice prevailed on his behalf.

Krista pushed her fear away and thought of Adan and Lyan. Alexi would never have sent men who looked like them, men who exuded the power and animal magnetism that they did.

She left the highway at the next off-ramp and pulled into a gas station. There were several other cars at the pumps, she scanned them, cautious even though she knew only sheer bad luck would lead to her being recognized here.

Krista steeled herself to make the phone call. By now she knew the number by heart, knew the DA's voice, though she didn't have a face to go with it.

"Is there a date yet?" she asked, not bothering to identify herself.

"Where are you?"

"Moving around."

"Krista, this is dangerous. Please, go to the nearest police station and I'll get you into the Witness Protection program."

"Is there a date yet?" she asked, willing to give him another chance to answer before she hung up. From the moment she'd reported the murder, she'd been unsure of who she could trust.

"No. These things take time. Look, Krista—"

"I'll call again," she said and hung up, afraid to stay on long enough to allow the call to be traced.

The phone started ringing immediately and pure fear whipped through her as she realized that he would guess her destination as soon as someone answered the phone and told him where it was located.

26

She lifted the receiver and heard the DA's voice. Without answering, she closed the connection. Even if she'd wanted to, there was no way to sever the phone cord. The best that she could do to delay the inevitable was to leave it off the hook and escape the area.

The adrenaline in her system surged and crested, threatening to make her physically sick. But finally it settled and she could think again.

If there was no trial date, then Alexi probably hoped to take her alive, to force her to marry him and live as a prisoner in his expensive house. Never talking to anyone on the phone, never seeing anyone other than those he allowed, never able to testify against him. His obsession was a curse and a blessing — without it she'd be dead.

Krista decided to return to Vegas. It was a big place, the best place to gamble without calling attention to her flair for mathematics, her better than average chance of winning. And if she saw Adan and Lyan again... Her heart squeezed in painful reaction and she shied away from thinking about them. There was no point in torturing herself. She had to concentrate on staying alive.

* * * * *

Adan and Lyan were not amused to find the dark-haired visitor waiting in their hotel suite after yet another day of visiting casinos and searching for their bond-mate. Already they had spent three horrific days in this gaming hell, but there had been no sighting of Krista.

Why are you here, Kye? Lyan asked. He made no effort to keep the unfriendly growl from his voice.

You wound me, cousin! The superior smile and uncontained amusement made a lie of his words. The visitor looked around. *I have come to see how you fair with your beautiful bond-mate. Where is she?* He frowned, his gaze swinging to encompass both Adan and Lyan. *I have never known either of you*

27

to drop your guard. Surely you weren't so overcome with lust that the Ylan crystals wavered and she saw your true form. When his comment was met with dual snarls, Kye relaxed and said, *True, she is a tiny thing, but not easily missed. Did you forget and leave her in the hallway?* He rose as if to go look for her.

Lyan growled, tense and ready to lunge for his cousin, more than willing to take some of his frustration out on Kye. Adan stepped forward, a buffer between the grinning Kye and the scowling Lyan. *Do you come on Council business or do you come to stir up trouble?* Adan asked.

Kye spread his hands wide. *One of the Council's scientists sent word that perhaps there was some mistake and the woman was not a true match since you have not returned with her nor have you been seen together after the first meeting. I volunteered to check on the matter. If she is not yours, then they will try for another bond-match. You know that she is too valuable to leave on this primitive planet.* He grinned at his cousin. *Though I have always favored the fire of red-haired women, your mate's hair shames the sun itself. Since you and I are of the same line, perhaps…*

Do not! Adan interrupted. *Or I will join Lyan in teaching you a lesson and it will be many months before you are useful to any female! She is ours. No one will take her from us.*

Kye grinned. *Truce, then. I can see the truth on my cousin's face…and other places. The mating fever of the Vesti rides him hard.* Slowly Kye's amusement faded and was replaced by honest concern. *What has happened with your mate? I ask now out of concern — for you as well as for your female. Was she offended by the thought of two mates? Are you sure the Ylan crystals did not fail? I have heard it said that some of the females can see us as we really are. I did not think she was one of them — but I am not her mate.*

Lyan gave a frustrated growl and stalked over to the bed. *We do not know, cousin. All seemed to be going well with Krista, then suddenly she snuck away from the restaurant and left us sitting like Ewellian fishermen on a dead sea.*

You did not mark her?

Lyan's growl was loud and savage. Kye cringed. *You did not.*

There was no opportunity, Adan said, then studied Lyan's cousin for a long moment. Kye was their equal in age and physical stature, but his emotions did not flare to the surface as Lyan's so often did. Like many of the men in Lyan's family, Kye was trained as a bounty hunter, a law keeper, as were the men of Adan's family. But unlike most of the Vesti, who still did not completely accept that the needs of all were best served by cooperation rather than fierce competition, Kye served the council that both governed and tried to help the various races survive genetic extinction after the Hotaling had let loose their bio-gene weapons.

A suspicion trickled across Adan's mind as he realized that Kye knew their mate was both tiny and blonde-haired. On rare occasions, when Council scientists feared they might lose track of a potential bond-mate, they sent one of their hunters to implant a tiny tracking-chip. It was done at a distance, with a special device, so that the female was not frightened or forewarned. The sting was no more painful than the bite of an insect and the chip was easily destroyed once she was claimed and mated.

Kye's presence suggested that there might be a way to salvage the situation, without the humiliation of going to the Council and admitting they had not secured their mate. Adan tried to still his rising excitement even as he considered which questions would lead them to Krista.

No male, much less one who was a bounty hunter, wanted to admit that his mate could so thoroughly elude him. But other than the sure knowledge that Krista belonged to them, they did not know enough about their mate to find her, especially if she fled the city as they feared she might eventually do.

Adan risked a quick glance at Lyan. His friend was now stretched out on the bed as though in meditation. Adan grimaced in sympathetic pain at the sight of the bulge pressing against the stiff uncomfortable fabric of Lyan's pants. The mating fever of the Vesti could lead to extreme pain as well as to extreme pleasure.

You have been to this planet before? Adan asked as he turned his attention to Kye.

Yes. The Council sent me six Earth-months ago.

To this city?

No. San Francisco, Los Angeles, Atlantic City, and finally New York. But there were many smaller places in between, many of them gaming hells such as this one. It was a very challenging job.

A potential bond-mate?

Yes.

You succeeded in the end?

Of course, though it was the most difficult hunt I have ever undertaken. There was no obvious logic in the travel patterns and I was hampered by our rules. He rolled his eyes. *The method of transport here is excruciatingly slow.*

So you have not been to this city before?

No. But that is no surprise. Most of the people you will encounter here are from elsewhere.

Adan's eyes narrowed. Kye smiled slightly.

You have not seen much of the city then? Adan asked.

No. Only a few casinos. None were memorable except for Gambler's Paradise. I drank in one of their smaller bars then enjoyed a wonderful meal there last night. Do you know it?

Adan's focus sharpened. It was the casino where they'd encountered their mate. It was the one place they were sure Krista was not. *Yes. But there are many restaurants in the casino. Which did you choose?*

Kye leaned back in his chair as though trying to remember. Adan laughed and shrugged. *It does not matter, perhaps the food is equally good throughout the casino. Lyan and I had an excellent meal of fajitas there.*

That dish sounds familiar. Perhaps it was the same place! Something they call Mexican.

Lyan and Adan were on their feet before Kye had finished the sentence. *You will be gone when we get back?* Lyan asked, his voice a low growl in his cousin's head.

Kye chuckled. *Yes. Though I have seen three males bonded to one female, I do not think this would be a good match.*

Adan shook his head at Kye's disregard for danger. But when Lyan would have turned back to do bodily harm to his cousin, Adan laughed and said, *I will enjoy taming our mate while you amuse yourself here.*

Lyan snarled at his cousin. *Make sure we are already bonded to our mate before we see you again.*

Kye grinned. *Of course, cousin. Perhaps I will visit your family and give your brothers news of your mate. I'm sure they will enjoy hearing tales of your conquest.*

Lyan's eyes narrowed. His teeth flashed when he snarled at Kye. Adan laughed. *Beware, Kye, perhaps even now the Council looks on Earth for your mate. Rest assured that Lyan and I will enjoy watching your pursuit and will take pleasure in seeing your mate bring you to your knees.*

Kye's laughter met his words. *That day will never arrive. From the moment my mate knows of my existence she will understand who she belongs to and will seek only to please me.*

Adan shook his head in disbelief. Lyan laughed out loud.

Before they could leave, Kye's expression grew serious and he halted Adan with a hand on his arm. "Your mother wishes you a speedy return from your quest. She worries for your brother. Zeraac has volunteered for another assignment, this one more dangerous than the last. She hopes that your return with a bond-mate and the promise of having nieces and nephews to help raise will give him a reason to embrace the future."

Pain shot through Adan at the mention of his older brother. He had seen the changes in Zeraac, and had feared for him. The Hotaling's virus had been a double curse, leaving his brother completely sterile and devastating him further when the woman he was pledged to had decided against the bond, preferring to join with another mate in the hopes that the scientists would somehow find a way for her to reproduce.

"Will you get word to Zeraac and ask him to stay until we return with Krista?"

Kye nodded. "I will go now."

Chapter Four

ဢ

Krista entered Gambler's Paradise for the fourth night in a row. She didn't expect to encounter Lyan or Adan, they'd probably decided a different casino better suited their tastes, or more likely, they'd returned home by now. It was just as well.

She'd accomplished what she needed to. She had enough money to keep moving and experience told her that she was now on borrowed time. It wouldn't be too long before someone spotted her and called Alexi.

Krista shivered. There had been several times during the last twenty-four hours when she felt as though someone was watching her. She hadn't seen anyone, and the watching somehow felt different than it had in other cities—not as menacing, but that could just be Las Vegas. This city shimmered with excitement and energy.

She ducked into one of the smaller casino bars to have a drink while the dinner crowd thinned at the Mexican restaurant. The bar was full, but not packed. She took a seat in the corner, where she could watch the door. Several moments later her heart leapt and awareness touched every nerve ending as Adan entered the bar.

Krista could almost believe that he was looking for her. His body tensed and his eyes scanned the room, finding her almost immediately. Their eyes met and she felt as though liquid heat was flowing into her heart, then traveling downward to her womb.

Her eyes flickered to the doorway, expecting Lyan to be right behind Adan. She felt disappointed when she didn't see him. It was hard to think of the one without the other, even though they seemed opposite in temperament.

Without hesitation, Adan headed straight to her. She tensed, guilty and anxious, excited but nervous. She owed him an apology. She prayed that she wasn't making a fatal mistake.

Adan's heart pounded in his chest as he drew close to Krista. Though the Amato had always been more flexible than the Vesti in their bonding arrangements, they were no less possessive of their chosen mates.

Now that Krista was within reach, he rode the thin edge of rage, pain, and desire. He wanted to put her on the table and shove his hard cock into her until she acknowledged who she belonged to. Until she swore that she would never torment him by running again.

He took a calming breath and sent word to Lyan. *I am with her.*

Heat seared back along their link, the same fierce desire that Adan was battling. *I am on my way.*

Krista couldn't tear her eyes away from the burning fierceness of his. He didn't ask permission to join her, but took the chair next to hers and immediately wrapped powerful fingers around her fragile wrist.

"I'm sorry," she whispered, barely able to squeeze the words out of her rapidly tightening chest. "I panicked when Lyan said you were bounty hunters."

The surprise of her words doused Adan's anger and eased some of his pain. Of all the things she might have said, he could not have anticipated—would never have anticipated—that it would be this. Bounty hunters—law keepers—were admired and respected in his world.

Adan could feel Lyan's sudden hesitation as he made his way to the bar. His friend's question echoed his own. "Why would you panic?"

Krista looked down at the table. As her finger traced the design on the cocktail napkin, she said, "I'm running from someone. It's not important who, just that I am. The last couple of places I've been, he found me by using private detectives."

She shrugged. "It wasn't much of a stretch to think he'd gone to bounty hunters when that didn't work."

Rage rushed thorough Adan. He would kill the man Krista was running from.

Only if you beat me to him, Lyan vowed and Adan could sense that Lyan was almost to the bar now.

Krista looked up then and added, "After I calmed down, I realized that you and Lyan probably hadn't been sent by…the person who's looking for me. So I came back. I hoped that I'd get a chance to apologize."

Adan cupped Krista's face with his free hand. "Tell me who this man is and I will take care of him so that he will never bother you again."

Krista laughed softly. "Thank you for trying to make me feel better. I won't bring you into my problems. Now that I've had a chance to apologize, I can move on with a clear conscience."

Lyan's growl roared through Adan's mind. Adan's hand tightened slightly as it cupped Krista's face, her eyes widened and flickered with the beginnings of fear.

"Never fear me," Adan said as he forced tension out of his body and gentleness into his voice.

A movement near the table caught Krista's attention. Her heart sped up in welcome when Lyan pulled a chair out and joined them.

"Who is this man who terrorizes you?" Lyan demanded.

Krista startled. How had he known there was a man? Suspicion began chasing her pleasure away.

Careful, Adan warned. *She is wary from being hunted. Let us not give her reason to run again.*

I will know who this man is!

We both will. But there is time. We must bind Krista to us first. The other can wait.

Lyan growled his acknowledgement then took Krista's free hand in his. With the added touch of his skin to hers, need whipped through her, demanding and fierce, making her nipples tighten and press against her thin blouse, causing an ache between her legs.

Both Adan and Lyan tensed in their chairs, almost overcome by the waves of lust washing over them. They did not require a mind-link to know the other's thoughts. Both ached with a need that was becoming urgent.

As the mating fever of the Vesti fought to overtake Lyan's control, he scrambled for something to say, something that would hasten the joining and end his torment.

Words had never come easily to him. He was a man of action, a man whose body spoke for him. Without a conscious decision he leaned forward and pressed his lips against Krista's.

Adan eased his hand from her face so that Lyan could take full possession. Lyan wasted no time in spearing his fingers through her silky blonde hair and holding her tightly to him. His tongued stroked against the seam of her lips, boldly demanding entrance. Krista groaned and complied.

The reality was better than any fantasy.

Krista was overwhelmed by Lyan's touch and taste. It was raw, primitive, as though he'd die if he couldn't merge his body with hers.

When the kiss ended, Krista was dazed and out of breath. Only slowly did the bar and its patrons come back into focus. Adan reached over and stroked a finger across her swollen lips. "Grant me the same favor Lyan has received." His voice was husky, aroused.

Krista licked her lips. Over the last three days she'd had a lot of time to think about what she might do if she encountered Adan and Lyan again. She was honest with herself—the curiosity, the fantasy, was part of the reason she'd returned to Vegas instead of moving on to Los Angeles or Reno.

She couldn't allow herself to believe that Alexi would eventually catch her. And yet a part of her, the cautious, conservative part that had kept her from living life to the fullest, from experimenting sexually, was now being overruled by a new desire to appreciate and squeeze every minute of pleasure that she could out of life.

Adan's eyes bored into hers. She pressed her lips against his fingers, wanting to say yes. But she was cautious, and shy, not wanting to make what was going to happen obvious to anyone who might be watching.

"Later," she whispered.

Adan's eyes narrowed. "Now. Return to our room with us."

Krista could feel his lust, his will pressing down on her. Heat stole across her face. She wanted to spend some more time with them before letting the chemistry take over. But it was dangerous. If they were seen with her… She swallowed hard, conscience warring with desire. The last man she'd gone out with had been involved in a hit-and-run accident. He survived, which was more luck than anything else. Only later did Krista learn that it was no accident.

Now the stakes were so much higher. She'd been blind to what Alexi was before the murder. She'd known he wanted to marry her and she was halfway to being in love with him. Going out with him had been like stepping into a whirlpool.

She'd been flattered by his attention, by the generous way he donated money to her school whenever she told him about a fundraising project. Even now she didn't know how she'd found the courage to slip back into the dining room and pretend that she hadn't witnessed Alexi pulling a gun from his pocket and firing it at point-blank range into the man who'd been forced to kneel in front of him.

She'd somehow managed to eat a piece of cake and drink her coffee, then pled an early night so that she would be fresh for helping her students prepare for their exams.

Alexi had allowed her to go home, but as soon as Krista had emerged from the police station, she'd been taken. Her stomach twisted at the memory of their confrontation, at her imprisonment, and the risk she'd taken to escape.

Only Alexi's desire to possess her had kept her alive this long. If she went with Adan and Lyan, Alexi would view it as yet another betrayal. If he found out, he'd probably kill them — and her, too. She shivered and tears formed as her nerve failed. She couldn't do this. She couldn't put their lives in danger.

Krista stared down at where Adan's fingers still held her wrist. She concentrated on his crystal-adorned wristband as she tried to regain her composure.

The fingers touching her lips moved to cup her chin and lift her face to Adan's. "We will not hurt you. Come with us."

"I can't," Krista said and at her other side, Lyan growled. She looked at him then. If anything, he looked more feral than when he'd first come into the bar. She licked her lips nervously. "I can't involve you in my life, not even for one night. The man I'm running from would kill you if he found out that you'd been with me."

Lyan snarled, baring his teeth as he did so. Krista paused to take a breath. She needed to say this, she had to make them understand. "The last man I dated got hurt because he'd gone out with me. Someone ran him down and nearly killed him. I didn't understand then, but now I do."

Adan stroked her palm. Lyan growled again. The rough sound in combination with the gentle caress tightened her nipples to hard points and made her shiver.

"You want us," Adan said, "and we do not fear this man you are running from. Let us take care of you, Krista. Come with us, find safety in our arms tonight."

The soft purr of his voice rubbed over Krista's body while the promise of what she craved most pierced her heart.

Adan leaned in and brushed his mouth against the sensitive skin below her ear. "Where we come from, bounty hunters are law keepers. Trust us." He took her earlobe between his lips, gently tugging before releasing it. "Let us take care of you."

Krista shuddered, unable to fight what they offered — what she needed — anymore. "Only for tonight. I need to leave tomorrow. It's not safe for me to stay any longer."

The two men rose from their chairs. Since each held one of Krista's wrists, she had no choice but to rise with them. She didn't fight it, her decision was made, but nervous energy and anticipation made the walk to their hotel and the elevator ride to their suite alternatively too short and too long.

Krista willed herself to relax as Adan shut the door behind them. The suite was large with two queen beds and plenty of floor space.

Lyan let her wrist go and sat on the closest bed. Krista's heart rate tripled as he took off his shirt and threw it on the dresser. His chest was covered in jet-black hair, his shoulders and back were smooth, the muscles flexing as he bent to remove his shoes.

Adan's arms circled Krista and pulled her against him. His lips trailed kisses down her neck. His erection pressed into her lower back.

Moisture coated her panties as Lyan stood and removed his pants. His erection rose hungrily against the firm flatness of his abdomen. She shivered and offered no resistance when Adan unzipped her jeans. But instead of pushing them down her legs, his hand slipped inside them, burrowing underneath her panties and through her silky pubic hair to cup her mound. She moaned as his fingers grazed her swollen clit and traced the wetness of her slit.

Lyan walked over and stopped in front of Krista. His mouth covered hers. His tongue stroked into her mouth as his hands made fast work of unbuttoning her shirt and unclasping the front of her bra. Krista shuddered and wrapped her arms around his neck, digging her fingers into his beautiful long hair.

Adan stroked a finger into her dripping vagina while his palm gave a quick press to her clit. Krista bucked and moaned into Lyan's mouth. One of Lyan's arms snaked around her shoulders and pulled her upper body against his chest. He palmed one breast, then ran his thumb over the nipple, rolling it before grasping and pinching it just as Adan pressed against her clit again.

Krista whimpered, beyond caring what they did to her as long as they kept bombarding her senses with exquisite pleasure. Adan bit gently where her neck and shoulder met, then stepped away. Immediately she missed the heat of him and would have pulled back to watch his movements except that Lyan's fingers slid down to her clit.

He circled around it several times, just barely touching it, then took it between his fingers and began pumping it in the same rhythm that his tongue was stroking against hers. She sobbed into his mouth and opened her legs wider as she ran her hands down his arms until she could clutch his sides. The beginnings of orgasm shimmered over her.

Lyan growled and plunged two fingers deep into her cunt while pressing his hand hard against her clit. He pulled his fingers back and she writhed against him, trying to follow them, not wanting to lose the pleasure his touch was bringing her. He plunged in again, this time with a long hard stroke to her clit and she couldn't hold on anymore. Orgasm tightened her inner muscles around his fingers and poured liquid desire into the palm of his hand.

Her body was still shuddering in release as Lyan rid her of her clothing then lifted her in his arms. Adan had pulled the mattresses off the beds and put them on the floor. He was naked except for the elaborately crafted wristbands, and every bit as masculine as Lyan.

Where Lyan was dark perfection, Adan was golden. His hair hung free, just below his shoulders, its color a rich honey.

His chest was smooth, the rich honey-colored hair absent until his groin.

Krista shivered in anticipation when she saw his erection. Already a drop of moisture glistened on its purple head.

They lay on either side of her. Adan took possession of her mouth while Lyan latched onto her nipple and sucked as though he wished he could pull milk from the pale pink bud.

Krista arched and sobbed. One hand tangled in Lyan's hair while the other hand traced down Adan's side until it could wrap around his cock. He bucked into her palm, groaning into her mouth when her thumb danced over the silky-soft head of his penis.

Lyan's lips moved down her chest to her soaking wet cunt. He nipped the soft swell of her abdomen, then the inside of her thigh before rubbing his tongue along her slit and over her clit.

Pure pleasure pulsed through Krista and she ran her thumb over the engorged head of Adan's penis in response. He jerked, sending more pre-cum to the throbbing tip.

"You are ours," he said as he shifted lower, biting then laving Krista's nipple. "You are ours to pleasure and protect."

Need, and lust, and something more—something so intense that it bordered on pain—surged through Krista like a hot wave as Adan stroked his tongue over her nipple and suckled in concert to Lyan's strokes and suckling of her clit.

Over and over again, they brought Krista to the edge then retreated. She strained to go over, she tried to wrap her legs around Lyan's head and force him to let her climax, but his hands easily gripped her thighs and held her open to him. She fought to push more of her breast into Adan's hot mouth, but he easily held her upper body pressed to the mattress.

"Please, Lyan," she whimpered as once again his mouth latched onto her clit and started sucking. Adan's lips left a burning trail across her chest as he switched breasts and took the sensitive nipple Lyan had already sucked into his mouth.

"Please, please," Krista cried, sobbing in desperation.

Adan raised his head and moved so that his face hovered only inches above hers. His pupils were completely dilated. "Do you accept what we offer?"

In some small rational part of Krista's mind, she wondered at the question, at the strange formality of it. But her body's demands left room for only one response. "Yes," she whimpered.

Lyan's tongue immediately plunged deep into her vagina and out again to lick her clit, bringing her to the razor edge of orgasm again. She sobbed when he pulled back. "Please, please."

Firm hands grasped and turned her over, positioning her so that she was on her hands and knees, vulnerable and open to Lyan while her mouth was just inches from Adan's throbbing cock.

With a deep growl, Lyan covered her and thrust his cock into her vagina. Krista moaned at his entry. He was so huge. He filled her as she'd never been filled.

When Lyan was completely in, he stilled, as though he wanted to savor this initial joining. Krista whimpered at the intense sensation.

He was hot, hard—a primitive male mounting his female. She arched her back, wanting to entice him, wanting him to pound into her, dominate her.

Lyan leaned closer, touching as much of his body to hers as he could. It felt as though a warm pelt covered her back.

His lips brushed against her neck. "You belong to us now. You are ours to pleasure and protect," Lyan said, repeating Adan's words before biting the tender skin at the base of her neck hard enough that Krista knew it was a demand for submission.

She dropped her head further and her lips brushed against Adan's throbbing cock. Krista had never wanted to go down on a man before, had never wanted to explore a penis with her lips and tongue. But now…now she wanted to give as much pleasure as she was receiving.

Adan's cock jumped as her lips and warm breath moved over it. "Krista," he groaned, and she responded by slowly tracing her tongue over the head of his engorged penis.

His breath caught in his throat and he lurched forward while one hand wrapped around his own cock. The sight was more than Krista could stand. She took everything above his fist into her mouth.

Lyan began moving in and out of her vagina and she began sucking Adan's cock in time to the thrusts. The pleasure was so intense, so all-consuming that Krista never wanted it to end, never wanted to be away from Adan and Lyan. She wanted to stay joined with them, pleasured by them, lost in this fantasy with them.

The hard, pounding thrusts into her wet tunnel increased in momentum. Lyan growled, pressing his chest even harder against her back, as though he wanted to melt right into her.

Krista cried out as his teeth pierced her soft flesh and ice-hot need radiated outward from the bite, lashing over her skin and making her writhe with pleasure so intense it was almost painful.

Adan groaned and arched. "Now," he growled and Lyan's fingers found Krista's clit.

Orgasm slammed into her, narrowing her focus to the pulsing cock deep inside her vagina and the straining shaft in her mouth. This time as pleasure roared through her, the men came with her.

It lasted forever.

And not long enough.

Krista was boneless with satisfaction. She made a little sound of protest when Lyan and Adan pulled away from her, but sighed in approval as they merely repositioned her body so that she was stretched out comfortably.

She'd been pleasured so thoroughly that she could barely keep her eyes open. And yet when Adan moved over her and Lyan's hand slid down her thigh to urge her legs apart, desire flared in her cunt—an ache that was too powerful to ignore. In that second she knew she wouldn't feel complete until Adan's seed was also deep in her womb.

When she opened her eyes, the expression on Adan's face was tender. She shifted, opening herself wider and offering him what he wanted. When he didn't immediately plunge into her, she whimpered and a satisfied smile flickered across Adan's lips.

He slid the very tip of himself into her opening then pulled back. Her vagina clenched, wanting to capture and hold him. He repeated the slow, torturous movement over and over again, never giving her more than a couple of inches.

Krista arched and whimpered. Her fingernails dug into his arms until he took her wrists in his strong hands and held them to the mattress. "What do you want?" he asked as her cunt squeezed desperately on his retreating cock.

"Fuck me, please fuck me."

His laugh was husky. "I am fucking you."

"Harder. Faster." She twisted underneath him, trying to force him into a deep thrust.

Adan's fingers tightened on her wrists, and he groaned as he fought her demand. "Admit you belong only to us."

She tightened on his cock again as it tunneled into her throbbing slit. "Yes."

"Say the words." He began to pull back and Krista sobbed.

"For tonight I belong only to you. To you and Lyan."

"For all time," Adan growled as his strokes became fierce, demanding, a male intent on mating his female. Krista echoed his movements, writhing and surging into him until her womb clamped down in victory, sending extreme pleasure shuddering through every nerve ending, through every cell, as it milked Adan of his seed. When she'd taken everything, he collapsed over her, pressing all of his weight on her momentarily before shifting over and cuddling her against him.

Lyan pressed against her other side. She felt his semi-rigid length against her and murmured, "Let me rest first," before drifting off to sleep. He chuckled in her ear, strangely content to just hold her. *She is everything I could have hoped for,* Lyan sent to Adan. *Tomorrow we can finish the claiming and take her home.*

Adan laughed softly. Amused enough to open his eyes and look at Lyan. *Do you truly believe it will be that easy?*

Lyan frowned. *You think it will be difficult? She has accepted our pledge and acknowledged that she belongs to us. Tomorrow she will be happy for us to take her away from what she fears.*

Adan laughed again. *Krista believes that she has given herself to us for tonight only. She does not truly accept that she is our bondmate, our wife. She will try and leave us tomorrow.*

Lyan snorted in disbelief. Among the Vesti it was unheard of for a female to try and leave after she'd been claimed and mounted. He stroked his tongue over the sheath hiding his mating fangs. It made his cock throb with remembered pleasure. Never before had the fangs slipped from their hiding place and pierced a female during the mating act. Never before had Lyan experienced the heightened pleasure of feeling the serum that helped bring about pregnancy and made a female easy to track, flow through his fangs at the moment of his climax.

She will not escape us, he growled in Adan's mind.

No, but she will try to leave us, to protect us from this man she fears. There was amusement in Adan's voice at Krista's innocent worry for their safety. But there was also steely resolve. She was theirs to pleasure and to protect. Adan would take great satisfaction in dealing with this man who dared to prey on Krista.

Only if you get to him first, Lyan growled in friendly challenge.

Chapter Five

ᔕ

Krista woke feeling warm and protected. She luxuriated in the feeling, savoring the absence of the fear that usually rushed over her the moment she came out of her sleep.

Lyan was pressed against her back, his hair-warmed chest a sensuous pelt against her bare skin. His arms were wrapped around her waist and his face nuzzled against the place where he'd bitten her.

She could hear the shower running. Adan.

Krista tried to ease away from Lyan. His arms tightened.

"I want to take a shower," she told him. He kissed her neck then released her.

Krista sat up and looked down at him. Even sleep-tousled, he was gorgeous.

Lyan grinned with male satisfaction. "Do you like what you see?"

She couldn't keep a small laugh from escaping. "I don't know. I'll have to think about it."

He pushed the covers away from his body. "What about now?"

Krista's gaze slid down the length of him, settling on his cock. It was already hard.

She wanted to take it in her hand, in her mouth. She wanted to see it grow even larger, even more desperate for relief. She wanted to feel it pounding into her.

It was all she could do to force her eyes away from it and back to his face.

Her body felt well-loved, tender even. But she knew she couldn't part from him without making love one more time.

"I need you again. But I want a shower first." Her voice sounded husky.

"Take your shower. But do not let Adan keep you too long or wear you out."

Krista rose and went into the bathroom. It was huge and luxurious. Plush rose-colored carpet cushioned her bare feet. A counter containing two sinks ran the length of one wall. Above it a mirror reached to the ceiling. Krista grinned as she caught her reflection. Well-loved was putting it mildly. She looked like she'd been ravished.

The door to the shower opened. Adan said, "Join me," and Krista covered the short distance and slipped under the hot, pulsing water with him.

Without a word Adan squeezed liquid soap onto his palms and began running his hands over Krista. She shivered and leaned into his smooth chest. "This is heaven," she murmured as he washed her body and then began on her hair.

When he finished with that, Adan moved his hands over her back and down to cup her buttocks. His erection throbbed against her abdomen.

Krista slid her hands down his sides and around to circle his penis and cradle the testicles that hung at its base. Satisfaction whipped through her at his groan, at the tensing of his body and the involuntary thrust into her hands.

With one hand she gently lifted and explored his balls, while the other slid up his penis and stroked near its engorged head. She couldn't resist the temptation to kneel down and take him in her mouth, to swirl her tongue over him. He bucked again and dug his hands into her hair, holding her to him. "You are playing with fire," Adan groaned.

Krista laughed and teased, "Good thing there's plenty of cold water here to put it out."

Adan gave a mock growl. "Water will not work on this fire."

"What will work?"

He didn't answer her with words but pulled her out of the shower. They stood in front of the mirror, with her back pressed against his front.

"Actions speak louder than words," Adan said. His voice was husky, aroused, more dominant now than playful. "I'll give you a demonstration of what works."

He slid his hands down her arms. When he got to her wrists, he took them and pulled them forward so that they braced against the counter.

Embarrassment and unwilling arousal made Krista's face flush as she looked at herself in the mirror, bent over with her breasts hanging and her legs spread in invitation.

Adan's hand slipped between her open thighs. His fingers dipped into her cunt, then over her already slippery clit. She moaned and started to close her eyes.

"No," Adan commanded. "Watch."

She watched as his fingers prepared her further, moving in and out of her body, working her clit, then sliding up to her hardened nipples, making them glisten with her own juices.

"You are so beautiful," Adan whispered. "You fill my soul as no other could. When I am near you, all I can think about is bringing you pleasure. All I want to do is lose myself in your body. You are meant to be mine, made for me, you are the only woman in the universe that can give me children. You are my bond-mate. Mine to pleasure and protect."

He squeezed her nipples one last time, then moved his hand down her body and buried his fingers between her thighs. "I can smell your arousal. It makes my balls ache and my cock throb. Nothing feels as good as being buried in your wet sheath." He plunged two large fingers into her slit and Krista could feel the walls of her vagina grip and pulse around them.

"When you do that to my cock it is all I can do to keep from spending myself the moment I am inside you." He panted as he began sliding his fingers in and out. "You threaten my control as no other has ever done."

Krista whimpered, arching her back and pushing against him. "Please, Adan, put your cock in me now."

His eyes dilated with pleasure and he stepped away from her so that she could see him in the mirror. "Look at what you do to me, Krista."

His cock was huge, engorged, dripping with his excitement. Krista met his eyes in the mirror and she made a small hungry noise before spreading her legs wider and arching her back to give him a better view of her swollen pussy.

Adan growled and moved to kneel behind her, running his teeth over her buttocks before maneuvering between her legs in order to suckle her clit. Krista cried, jerking away from the touch that was so much pleasure it bordered on pain.

He grabbed her hips and held her to him as his tongue darted into her slit, then out again in order to lap up her juices. "I want you to ache like you make me ache," he said. "I want you to need like I need."

Krista sobbed. "Oh god, you're killing me, Adan. Please, please finish it."

He repositioned himself in order to see her face. When she started to close her eyes he nipped her buttock. "Watch then. Watch while your bond-mate takes you."

Adan stood and guided his thick cock into her from behind. His face tightened and flushed as he began pounding into her so deep and hard that she could hear and feel his sac swinging against her puffed cunt lips.

Krista writhed against him, pressing into him, crying out like an animal in heat. She was beyond any thought other than the need to climax and bring her mate to completion.

Adan rode her to orgasm. Only then did Krista's eyes close, but when he gave one last savage thrust and groaned in release, Krista opened them and watched his pleasure as he filled her with his seed.

They stood for a few minutes, both panting, both too weak to move. Finally Adan pulled out of her and together they returned to the shower for a quick rinse.

Before they finished, the shower stall opened and Lyan stepped in. "I was afraid that there would be no more hot water by the time you two were done."

Adan chuckled and gave Krista a quick kiss before leaving the shower. Lyan took her into his arms, pressing his already hard cock against her in a bid for attention.

Krista wrapped her arms around Lyan's neck and laughed. "Poor baby."

"Put your hands on my shoulders and wrap your legs around me," Lyan said as he easily lifted her.

Krista did as he wanted and was immediately rewarded. His cock sank into her in one thrust. She hadn't realized how much she needed it until it was there—hot, hard, filling her.

Lyan turned so that her back was against the smooth, cool, shower wall while her front was covered by hot man and warm spray. "Just a quick one now, to start the day," he said, then began tunneling in and out of her in a surprisingly gentle movement. His lips covered hers and his tongue mimicked what his cock was doing.

Even when her inner muscles gripped and pulled at him as she climaxed, Lyan did not stop kissing her until the last of his cum had been pulled from his testicles.

"I will never get enough of you," he said against her lips before stepping away and reaching for the soap.

Reality returned like a painful fist squeezing Krista's heart. If things were different… Maybe one day… She shook the thoughts away. Nothing had changed. This was a fantasy, one she'd never leave if she truly had a choice. But there was no choice. She was on the run and anyone with her was at risk.

She quickly rinsed and escaped the shower. When she entered the bedroom, she found her clothes. The shirt and jeans were wrinkled, but decent until she could get to her car. Preferring to go without yesterday's panties, she jammed them into the pocket of her jeans.

Adan sat on the bed, also dressed. When she looked at him, he smiled. "We will go get something to eat."

Krista crossed the room and sat down next to him. "As soon as Lyan comes out of the bathroom, I need to leave."

Adan laughed softly and pulled her onto his lap. Though his touch was gentle, the arms around her were like steel bands. "You belong to us now. You are ours to pleasure and protect. Our bond-mate."

Krista shook her head, trying to keep her mind clear and fight off the fantasy she'd been caught in. "Please don't make this more difficult than it is. We both know this is a…"

She couldn't bring herself to say one-night stand. Though she'd never had one before, what she'd experienced with Adan and Lyan felt like something more than that, better than that.

Taking a deep breath, she continued. "I can't stay. Not here. Not anywhere. Maybe one day, if you haven't found someone else…"

He stopped her words with a gentle kiss. "There is no one else for us. We will not let you go."

Tension flowed into Krista. As male as they were, she should have known that the challenge of defeating another man would only get their testosterone raging.

"You don't have a choice."

Adan's face hardened but whatever words he might have said were stilled as Lyan walked into the room.

The fight begins, Adan said in Lyan's mind, *as I said it would. She seeks to leave us.*

Lyan growled low in his throat and began to dress. *This is foolishness. The Council rules only delay the inevitable. She is ours. Whether she acknowledges it before or after we take her home matters not.*

Adan shrugged. *Foolish or not, unless the rules are obeyed, the Council has the right to set aside the bond.*

Violent images played through Lyan's mind, most involving the Council members. Adan chuckled then stood, easily lifting Krista with him and setting her on her feet. "We should go eat before Lyan loses all control of himself."

Krista stiffened, prepared to argue, but then thought better of it. Though she would prefer not to run from them as she had before, if it became necessary to do so, then it would be more easily done from a public place. She would not have their deaths on her conscience. Still, she couldn't resist saying, "I have to leave after we eat."

Adan gave a half-smile. "We can discuss it once we have refueled."

Krista shook her head, this time not giving in to the temptation to continue the argument.

They ate in one of the casino restaurants. Krista chose to make it breakfast and ordered French toast even though their waitress told them that it was past noon.

Time in Las Vegas was meaningless. But Krista knew that was an illusion she couldn't afford. The closer she got to finishing her meal, the edgier she'd become, as though some survival instinct was kicking in. *Leave*, it whispered. *Leave now.*

Krista looked around the restaurant. There was nothing obvious. No one obvious. But that didn't mean she hadn't been spotted by someone who knew that Alexi was looking for her.

She put down her fork and pulled some money out of her pocket. "Thank you both for a wonderful time. But I really do have to go."

Adan chuckled and took her hand in his, trapping the bills against her palm. "It is our right and duty to give you pleasure, there is no need for you to pay us." He grinned. "The satisfaction we received was payment enough. Is that not so, Lyan?"

Lyan took her other hand. As always, a current of need whipped through Krista, arcing between the places where they touched her.

"No other can give us what you can, Krista," Lyan said.

Adan moved closer and whispered, "Tell me that you can not feel the bond that ties the three of us together. Tell me that you do not feel the rightness of it."

"Don't make this harder than it already is," Krista pleaded. Her voice breaking, a revelation of the feelings that fluttered through her heart.

"Tell us about this man you fear so much," Adan urged.

"No. It's better if you're not involved."

Lyan growled. Adan chuckled. "We are already involved. Perhaps even now he thinks to challenge us for possession of what is ours."

Krista shivered, aroused by his continued assertions of ownership, but wary, too—for herself, for them, of them. They were so outside the range of her experience.

"Tell us just a little bit," Adan coaxed.

"Then you'll let me go without making it harder for me?"

"Yes."

No! Lyan protested.

Adan's glance slid to Lyan. *You have marked her in the way of the Vesti—she cannot elude us again. She is like a ginka-bird, craving a safe place to land and build a nest, yet wary of being trapped and confined. If we wish to hold her to us, then it must be with an open hand and not a closed fist.*

Frustration seethed through Lyan as Krista's gaze turned to him. He could see the wariness overlaying the beginnings of their mate-bond. He could hear the ring of truth in Adan's words. Yet it went against the nature of his people to let a mate escape. It went against *his* nature. The mating fever of the Vesti drove a male to mate his female until she acknowledged his dominance and accepted his protection, until she craved his touch as much as he needed hers.

To Adan he said, *I will trust your judgment, but should something happen to threaten her, then she will be bound in the way Vesti-mates have always been bound.*

Krista placed her free hand on Lyan's. "Do you agree?"

"Agreed."

Adan asked, "What does this man wish to do with you, Krista?"

She shivered as memories of her escape washed over her. Alexi hadn't anticipated that she would risk drowning in order to get away from him. Nor had he factored in the number of boaters who might pass close enough to his anchored yacht, boaters who could give her a ride to shore.

Krista licked her lips in a nervous gesture and could almost taste the salt of the ocean on them. Alexi wouldn't underestimate her again. Next time he'd leave nothing to chance—if he didn't kill her first.

"He'd take me somewhere and no one would ever see me again."

Lyan's growl was deep and savage. "He would kill you?"

"Maybe not right away. But eventually." Her stomach churned, queasy now at the memory of how she'd once slept with Alexi.

Krista shivered. She wouldn't be able to bear his touch again, much less touch him.

Adan reached over and stroked the side of her face. "Come home with us. We can protect you from him."

"There's nowhere on Earth that he can't eventually reach me. He's wealthy and well-connected." She turned so that her lips brushed against Adan's palm. "You don't know how much your offer means to me. But I can't, absolutely won't, put you and Lyan in danger. Al— The man I'm running from would kill you for offering me shelter alone. If he thought you were my lovers, it would only make him that much more determined to destroy you and anything you cared about."

Krista shook her head. "I've made myself crazy looking back and seeing if there were warning signs that I should have noticed. Maybe someone with more experience would have known. But I didn't realize what kind of a man he was until it was too late." Unexpected tears formed at the corner of her eyes as the image of Adan or Lyan being mowed down by a speeding car, as her friend Matt had been, flashed through her mind. "I couldn't stand it if something happened to either of you because of me."

Fierce, unfamiliar emotions swirled through Lyan at the sight of her tears, at the caring in her voice. He wanted nothing more than to pick her up and take her back to the home he and Adan had prepared for her. "Trust us to protect you," he pleaded, shocked that he'd been reduced to such tenderness. "Come home with us."

Krista shook her head. "No. I can't." There was a catch in her voice as she pulled her hands away. "I should leave now. The longer I wait, the harder it'll be."

Lyan wanted to argue. He wanted to demand that she yield. But he'd given his word. For now she would get what she thought she must have.

Adan said, "We will escort you to your car." His voice was firm, leaving no room for argument. Krista nodded her head in acceptance.

Chapter Six

ಬ

Kye d'Vesti watched in amazed disbelief as Lyan and Adan calmly walked their bond-mate to her car and allowed her to drive away.

That Krista was their mate was not in doubt. Even without witnessing the possessive way they hovered around her, Kye could see the mark Lyan's mating fangs had left at the base her neck.

He shook his head, bemused, almost forgetting himself and making his presence known. No doubt if he was foolish enough to be seen, his cousin would use it as an excuse to pound out some of his frustration.

Despite Lyan's warnings, curiosity had led Kye to return after delivering Adan's message to Zeraac, but now he could justify his continued observation as part of his duty to the Council. After all, hadn't he been charged with the task of tracking and tagging Krista so that she could be claimed by her mates? And since she still had the implanted tracking device, surely it was reasonable to assume that he was supposed to continue monitoring the situation. After all, Earth females were too valuable to risk.

Kye grinned. He was going to enjoy teasing his rough cousin in the years to come. How the mighty had fallen! And at the hands of such a tiny female!

He chuckled as he watched Adan and Lyan hurry back to their hotel, and the slow Earth transport that they were required to use. If Lyan were alone, then Kye knew that his cousin would disregard the Council's orders as he so often did and travel as he pleased. But the Amato were sticklers for following the rules, and Adan was no exception. He would keep Lyan in check in order to ensure that there was no challenge to the bond.

Kye prepared to follow Krista, using technology that was forbidden, but so much faster. He shook his head one last time in amazed disbelief as he watched the two warriors disappear. When the time came for him to mate, he would not let his female lead him on such a chase!

* * * * *

Krista's heart ached as she drove away from Adan and Lyan. She didn't want to leave them, but she didn't have a choice.

She sniffed, trying to keep from actually breaking down and crying. God! Why did she have to meet them now?

Her chest squeezed painfully and she wiped stray tears off of her cheeks. This was pathetic, she'd gotten caught up in a fantasy, that's all. This wasn't real life. This was Vegas!

She was a vacation fling for them, and they were an escape from all the pent-up stress of being on the run. That's all it was. She didn't doubt their sincerity when they said they wanted to protect her. They'd been just as caught up in the fantasy as she'd been.

But real life wasn't something called a mate-bond between a high-school math teacher and two men who could have stepped off the covers of a romance novel.

Real life was one husband—if you could find someone you'd even like to marry. Krista wiped at a few more tears. It wasn't even legal to be married to more than one man at the same time!

A fist tightened around her heart. Real or not, it had felt so right. She'd never be able to find someone like Adan or Lyan.

Just thinking about them and the intense sex they'd shared had her body throbbing with need all over again. She took one hand off the steering wheel and ran it over the hard pebble of her nipple and down to her cunt, rubbing her clit though the thick material of her jeans.

It wasn't enough and she had the horrible premonition that it would never be enough. They'd ruined her for other men. They'd even ruined her for herself!

Krista took a long shuddering breath and reached for the radio. After the first sad song about lost love and heartbreak, she turned it off. She didn't need that!

Finally she resorted to playing blackjack in her head as she drove. And every time an image of Adan or Lyan popped into her mind, she made herself play three imaginary hands plus the dealer's at the same time. That kept her busy until she got to the outskirts of Reno.

Reno should be okay, at least for a few days. She'd stop by and visit Savannah. That was always fun. And it should be safe enough, especially if Savannah was in uniform. Even Alexi's goons wouldn't be stupid enough to try and kidnap her in front of a cop.

She would see if the cabin was empty. If it was, then she could stay there, out of sight for a while. Krista felt some of the tension leave her with the decision. Yeah, that's what she needed, a distraction and a chance to be surrounded by nature. When her parents were alive they'd often stayed at the cabin owned by Savannah's family.

Thank God she'd never mentioned it to Alexi—never mentioned Savannah or Reno. It'd be a good place to hide out for a little while.

Krista smiled in anticipation as she pulled into a convenience store parking lot and placed a call to the police station. She was in luck. Savannah's shift had just ended.

"Do you remember where that hole-in-the-wall place called The Dive is?" Savannah asked.

Krista laughed. "You know I do. That's the only place in town that used to let us in with our obviously fake IDs when we were sixteen."

"I'll take the fifth on that," Savannah laughed. "Why don't you meet me at The Dive? It's a safe enough place these days and as soon as I change clothes I'm heading there anyway. I'm supposed to meet a snitch but my business with him shouldn't take too long."

Krista smiled. Savannah hadn't changed a bit. She was all cop, all the time.

"See you there," Krista said and hung up the phone.

For a brief second her nerve endings warned that she was being watched. It was the same sense of watching she'd had in Las Vegas—curious instead of threatening, benevolent instead of malicious. Krista hastily looked around. Every car in sight was occupied by people with gray hair or people with children.

She rubbed her arms and returned to her car. As far as she could see, no one followed her out of the parking lot and to the meeting place. Still, Krista took the added precaution of staying in her car, intending to wait for several minutes before going into The Dive.

When a silver pickup truck pulled into the parking lot, Krista's spirits lifted and she laughed out loud. Some things never changed. Savannah's truck had more dents and dings in it than it did smooth surface. It looked like her friend still went after the stray cows on her parent's ranch with the same kind of gusto she went after criminals.

Krista left her car and hurried over to give the red-haired dynamo climbing out of the truck a hug. Savannah returned the hug.

"Sorry I'm late." Savannah's lips turned downward in a grimace, though the sparkle in her eyes told Krista that whatever Savannah was getting ready to say, she was more amused than upset by it. "The captain had to give me my weekly dressing-down about investigating while off-duty."

Krista laughed. "As in meeting a snitch tonight?"

Savannah rolled her eyes. "Don't even go there! With any luck the captain won't find out about it." She checked her watch. "We might as well go in. The Ferret will know where to find me."

"The Ferret?"

"Looks like a weasel, smells like a weasel, and acts like a weasel—so I call him The Ferret, though I think his real name is something like Dale or Ricky."

Krista shook her head and laughed. Savannah was terrible with real names, but she was great at nicknaming people.

They went inside and took a back booth, which suited Krista. It gave her a great view of the door and no way for anyone to sneak up on them.

"So what brings you to Reno?" Savannah asked after the waitress had taken their orders.

Krista looked at her friend and wished she could tell her about Alexi. But that was impossible. Telling Savannah would be as bad as telling Adan and Lyan. Maybe even worse. Savannah would go after Alexi even if it put her own job and life in jeopardy.

"I thought it'd be nice to get away for a while, maybe use the cabin if it's available." It sounded lame even to Krista.

Savannah's expression said she didn't believe it for a second. But Krista was spared the agony of immediately undergoing an interrogation when their drinks and nachos arrived.

After the waitress left, Savannah pounced. "Man trouble?"

Krista's mind flashed first to Alexi, but quickly moved to Adan and Lyan. In a moment of insight, she realized that right now the ache of leaving them, of not exploring whether the fantasy could be a reality, was more agonizing than the fear she had of Alexi.

Some of what she was feeling must have shown on her face. Savannah shook her head and said, "Oh boy, you have it bad. Want to tell me about the asshole who broke your heart? Maybe he's got an outstanding warrant or something and I can make sure the wheels of justice turn."

Krista laughed. "What you really mean is, make sure the wheels of justice roll over the guy and flatten him."

Savannah grinned. "That, too." Then on a more serious note she added, "Feel free to use the cabin for as long as you need to. I'm all ears if you want to talk."

Krista took a deep breath. She couldn't talk about Alexi, but would it hurt to talk about Adan and Lyan? She and Savannah had been friends forever. They hadn't grown up together in a three-hundred-and-sixty-five-days-a-year manner, but every time Krista's family had come to stay at the cabin, she and Savannah had been inseparable. Some years their togetherness had lasted more weeks than in other years, but no matter how long it had been between visits, it always seemed like it was just yesterday that they'd been together. The two of them had clicked and kept on clicking.

Krista cleared her throat and reached for a nacho. She could feel heat rising to her face as she mumbled, "It's not just one guy, it's two. And they didn't break my heart exactly." She stopped, not knowing how to continue. Finally she said, "I want to be with them, but I can't."

Savannah grabbed a nacho and dug it into the pot containing the hot cheese. "Oh boy. Are you talking both at the same time, or two different boyfriends in two different locations?"

"Both at the same time."

Savannah made a show of waving air onto her face. "Is this your idea or theirs?"

Krista's blush deepened. "We're all okay with it."

"I am speechless."

"That's a first," Krista mumbled.

Savannah grinned. "Yeah, my captain would say that, too." Her face went somber. "So what's holding you back? Are you afraid it'd get back to your principal and you'd get canned on a morals clause?"

Krista's heart lurched and plummeted. She'd been so focused on keeping Adan and Lyan safe that she hadn't given any thought to the bigger picture. But Savannah was right.

She didn't know where Adan and Lyan lived, but even though San Francisco was pretty liberal, parents at her school still kicked up a fuss over gay out-of-the-closet teachers. They'd be apoplectic about a teacher who openly lived with two men. And remembering the way Lyan had kissed her in the bar, and Adan's demand to also share a kiss, plus their possessive behavior in the restaurant, Krista knew that there was no way a relationship with them would remain hidden. Not that she'd ask that of them—or herself.

She swallowed hard and said, "Yeah, something like that."

Savannah reached for her arm and gave a little squeeze. "So go on a trip somewhere and enjoy the fantasy. That's what I'd do."

Surprise chased across Krista's face and Savannah laughed. "What, you don't think I have fantasies, too?" Her eyebrows went up and down in a comical manner. "I have a very active imagination."

Krista laughed. "So you'd take on two guys at once?"

"Oh yeah. And I'd bring out the lariat."

"No!"

Savannah grinned. "You know how much I love to rope and tie things. Now tell me about these two guys." And Krista did.

When she got finished, Savannah said, "Stop. Do not pass GO. Do not collect your two hundred dollars. Tell me if they have any gorgeous friends, then find a room and lock the three of you in it!"

Feeling more lighthearted than she had since this thing with Alexi began over a year ago, Krista laughed and said, "I take it there aren't any fantasy men in your life right now."

"Not even close. The only guys I see are cops and crooks—not exactly prime candidates in the relationship department."

"What about the cowboys on your parents' ranch? The way I remember it, that's where all the great-looking guys could be found."

Savannah rolled her eyes. "Now that my brothers have taken over so my parents can travel, any guy they catch looking my way gets to check fences. I've been told that riding the fence line with a raging hard-on is very painful. These days all I have to do to clear a room of cowboys is to walk into it! And yeah, you're right—the Bar None bunkhouse is still full of eye candy."

Krista snickered. "So close and yet so far away."

"You've got that right," Savannah said as she checked her watch and frowned.

"Is your snitch late?" Krista asked.

"Yeah, by about ten minutes. The Ferret is the nervous type. He usually arrives early, lurks in the shadows until he makes sure it's safe, then slinks out. It's not like him to be late." She rose from her chair. "I think I'll check outside, just in case."

Krista stood up too. Since she'd started running from Alexi, she'd learned to listen to her instincts and right now they were screaming at her not to let Savannah go outside alone. "I'll go with you."

"No way, this is police business."

"Official police business?" Krista asked with a raised eyebrow.

Savannah shook her head ruefully. "That's the trouble with confessions—they always come back to haunt you. Come on. These days The Dive is a pretty quiet place. I don't really expect trouble. The Ferret probably got a better offer and that's why he's a no-show, but I'd kick myself if I found out later that he was hanging around outside."

"What kind of information is he selling?"

"I don't know."

"You don't know!"

Savannah grimaced. "All he said was that it was something big. Something big enough that if I break it wide open, the brass will have to give me a detective shield, and my days as a beat cop will be over."

Alarm bells were practically shrieking in Krista's head as they stepped out of the bar and Savannah said, "That looks like The Ferret's car."

The car was parked down the street, on the other side of an alleyway. The brand new black Beemer was one of the expensive models. It told Krista that the information business paid well. "This feels bad," she said, looking around at The Dive's parking lot. It was practically empty. "Why didn't he park here?"

Savannah's smile sent terror straight to Krista's heart. "I don't know. But there's one way to find out."

Chapter Seven
ഇ

Kye's cock came to a rapid and throbbing attention when he saw the flame-haired woman step out of the bar with Krista. By the stars, she was the one. She was his mate.

He did not need the Council and its scientists to confirm it. The blood pouring into his shaft, the fire racing through his veins, the need that made him want to leave his hiding place and stride over to claim her were all the proof he needed. She was his.

She was also armed and dangerous.

Kye shook his head as though to clear the images being transmitted from his eyes to his brain. Had his mate just pulled one of their primitive weapons from a holster at her side? Was she even now moving away from him in the manner of a hunter tracking prey?

She was.

Kye didn't know whether to laugh or to yell in rage as he quickly determined a destination and transported to it. Now that he'd found his mate, there was no way that he would allow anything to happen to her.

* * * * *

Krista was not one to play cops and robbers. Never had been, never would be. Teaching high-school math in a public school was dangerous enough for her tastes, though in all honesty, teaching in a magnet school for high achievers didn't exactly put her in any great jeopardy.

"Shouldn't you call for backup or something?" she whispered to Savannah.

Savannah shook her head but didn't turn to say anything as she moved along the building and edged toward the alleyway.

Krista took a deep breath and tried to calm down. It felt like warning bells were still clanging away in her skull.

Savannah held up a hand to signal a halt, then crouched low with her gun in the ready position as she prepared to go around the corner.

This is crazy! Krista thought. *I'm not even armed!*

Savannah eased around the alley and Krista tensed, half expecting to hear gunfire erupt. It was almost a letdown when it didn't.

"All clear," Savannah said as she stood up and holstered the gun.

Krista moved to look into the alley. Savannah was right. It was clear from one end to the other—no junked cars, no metal trashcans or cardboard boxes, no dumpsters hugging the building walls, no bad guys waiting to ambush them. Krista breathed a sigh of relief and tried to relax. But her instincts wouldn't let her drop the protective guard that had kept her ready for trouble all of these months. A car started down the block and sent her pulses racing, though there was nothing suspicious about it. It eased away from the curb and began moving in the opposite direction.

"I still don't like this," Savannah said, eyeing The Ferret's car. "I've got a feeling that I'm not going to like what's in the Beemer either." She took a step forward.

In her peripheral vision Krista saw the car at the end of the block hesitate at a corner. The back window opened several inches. A flash caught Krista's attention as the sun struck something emerging from the window. Instinct more than anything else had her grabbing Savannah and pulling her into the alley.

"What the—" Savannah got out before an explosion filled the air, rocking the buildings around them and knocking them to the ground. Glass rained down from nearby windows, along with pieces of brick and black Beemer.

Krista was so stunned that it took her several seconds to notice the man who'd suddenly appeared and crouched down next to them. He looked so much like Lyan that she gasped.

* * * * *

Until this moment, Kye had never felt the primitive emotions that so often overtook Vesti males. But now, as he looked down at his debris-covered mate, they poured through him.

He wanted to find whoever had done this to her and make them pay — slowly and painfully. He wanted to carry his mate home and ensure that her life was never in danger again.

Kye's eyes traveled to Lyan's mate and love for her swelled in his heart. If not for her, his own mate would be dead.

"Lyan?" Krista asked, frowning in puzzled confusion.

"No, I am Kye."

Krista shook her head to clear it and slowly sat, her attention going to her friend. "Savannah, are you okay?"

Savannah groaned and sat up. "Yeah, nothing that some Advil and hydrogen peroxide won't take care of." She brushed a hand over her hair, sending small pieces of glass and brick to the concrete. "Man, I knew I wasn't going to like what was in that Beemer!"

Her grin sent a wave of fury through Kye. Did his mate not realize that someone had been waiting for her? Was trying to kill her?

Krista shook her head and shuddered. "Maybe you should leave town for a while, Savannah. Somebody set you up."

Savannah rubbed her hands together. "Where there's smoke, there's fire. This could be my big break. What'd you see before the explosion? What tipped you off?"

Krista told her.

Kye's nostrils flared with suppressed fury. The purple crystals in his wristbands swirled and pulsed as his emotions threatened his control. The need to take his woman and get her to safety was almost overwhelming. "Who wants to hurt you?" he demanded.

Green fire flashed in his mate's eyes and sent blood roaring to his cock. When he got her away from here, she would feel the sting of his hand on her ass before he mounted her.

"And you are?" his defiant mate—Savannah—had the nerve to ask in a challenging tone.

"Kye d'Vesti, cousin to Lyan d'Vesti."

Savannah's eyes grew round and her lips formed a small o. To Krista she said, "Wow."

Krista flushed with heightened color. "Did Lyan and Adan send you? How did they know I was here?"

Kye answered, "Lyan does not yet know where you are. He told me of you and I was curious so I followed you here from Las Vegas."

Krista stiffened. "Why were you curious?"

Kye grinned. "It is not every day that my fierce cousin is brought to his knees. I wanted to see the female who had tamed him." He shook his head. "Be warned, once Lyan returns to his senses, he will come after you."

"Are you going to tell him that I'm here?"

The range of emotions warring on Krista's face—the longing and despair—made Kye more curious than ever as to what was going on between Adan and Lyan and their beautiful bond-mate, but he shook his head and set her mind at ease by saying, "No, you have my word that I will say nothing to him."

Of course, he had no need to tell his cousin. The serum Lyan injected into Krista's bloodstream when he sank his mating teeth into her had forged a connection that allowed him to sense where she was. It also allowed Lyan to reach her mind and retrieve her location from it as soon as she was lost in sleep. Once claimed, it was impossible for a Vesti mate to escape.

A siren sounded in the distance. Savannah scrambled to her feet. "Damn, we need to get out of here. Let's go out the alley and around. The fewer people that see us, the better."

Krista frowned. "Shouldn't you stick around and make a report or something?"

"Trust me, it'll do more harm then good if my captain gets word of this. And until I know more about what's going on, I'm going to play this one close to the chest. The Ferret said he was onto something big. I don't know how long it's going to take for them to find out who the car belonged to, but I need to get to The Ferret's place and see if there's something there that'll help me make sense of this thing."

"I'll go with you," Krista said, following Savannah to the end of the alley and around the corner.

Savannah shook her head. "No. It'd be safer if you didn't. Please, go to the cabin. I'll call you to let you know I made it home."

Krista's face grew determined. "I'm not letting you go by yourself. I'm going, even if I have to wait in the car."

Kye ground his teeth together. His mate would soon learn that putting herself in danger was unacceptable. Despite his promise to Krista, he sent out a mental probe to determine if Lyan and Adan were near. Relief washed through him when he found that they were rapidly approaching the city. Soon they would be here to take charge of their mate.

Kye and the two women slipped into The Dive's parking lot unnoticed. A crowd was gathered around the remains of the black Beemer down the street. As Savannah used the remote on her key chain to unlock the doors of her pickup, Krista said, "I'm not letting you go alone. I'll follow you in my car."

"No," Kye said. There would be hell to pay if he allowed something to happen to Lyan and Adan's mate. "I will go with Savannah."

Savannah stiffened. "I don't believe you were invited."

Kye's attention was immediately drawn to his mate. He took her arm and tried to retrieve the keys. When she didn't yield, he pulled her against his body. The smell of her filled his nostrils and imprinted itself on his soul.

"Back off," she growled, trying to escape his arms.

Savannah's struggles only served to press her hard-tipped breasts against his chest. He smiled. She was not immune to him. But if looks could kill, his mate would even now be facing charges for his murder.

"No. We have much to discuss." Kye didn't bother to keep the growl out of his voice as he forced the keys from her grasp, then opened the door and urged his mate into the truck. Once she was inside, he turned to Krista and cupped her face in his hand. "You have my word that I will keep your friend safe. She is my bond-mate. Those who would harm her will pay with their lives."

Krista's eyes widened. Kye smiled and pressed his lips to hers, sucking and teasing until she opened her mouth to him. His tongue rubbed over hers, offering comfort and reassurance. When the kiss ended, Kye said, "Leave now. Do not worry for your friend."

Chapter Eight

ක

"If our mate truly cared for our comfort, she would stay in one of the hotels instead of in a cabin," Lyan muttered as he swatted yet another of the flying insects that seemed to favor his blood over Adan's.

Beside him, Adan moved easily, rubbing his back against the tree he was leaning on. *If our mate knew we were watching her, there would be hell to pay.*

As though we do not already pay! Lyan slapped at another of the winged pests. The separation from Krista had left him constantly hard and as each day passed, he cared less about the rules and more about securing their mate. What insanity had overcome him? His brothers would never let him live it down should they find out that he had willingly let his mate leave—had even walked her to her car and given her a kiss goodbye!

It was insanity! He had been a fool to let Adan's reasoning and Krista's tears sway him. One more insect bite and he was going to climb down to the cabin below!

* * * * *

Krista stood on the porch and took a deep breath as she looked around. She'd been twenty, on the verge of twenty-one, the last time she'd camped here. It was the summer before her last year at college. Her parents had said they wanted her all to themselves one last time before she left the nest.

Back then she thought they were being overly dramatic, not that she minded camping with them. They were a close family, just the three of them.

She'd rolled her eyes and teased them for making graduating from college sound like she was dropping off the face of the Earth. But what had she known back then? She'd been full of youthful enthusiasm and unrealistic expectations. Yes, she'd be living away from home, but the great thing about teaching was the summer break. She'd still be back during the summer and for vacations. Life wasn't radically changing, just evolving.

But of course, her life was changing, and the changes took place rapidly once she'd graduated and started her first job. New friends. New adventures. New experiences. New challenges.

She'd gone back home and visited, but it was never the same. And then there was no home to go back to.

Her parents had been killed in a plane crash along with a pilot friend of theirs and his wife. They'd been on their way to Colorado when their small plane got caught in a storm.

Krista rubbed her hand over her heart. The ache was still there even after all these years.

She turned her mind to Savannah, wondering how she was doing with Kye and whether Savannah was getting to experience her fantasy of being with two men at once. Kye had been alone, but he'd claimed that Savannah was his bond-mate. Krista assumed that meant a shared-mate in his case as well.

Her eyebrows drew together and her heart sped up as she thought about it now. Kye had used the word bond-mate so naturally, as though the concept of a shared-mate was perfectly normal. And his speech was formal...old world, as Adan and Lyan's were. She still didn't know where home was for them. Was it possible that they lived in a tightly knit community where it was acceptable to have more than one husband...or wife?

Krista frowned. Sharing a man with another woman was *not* one of her fantasies.

She shrugged the worry away. Despite Kye saying that Lyan and Adan would find her, she didn't see how that was possible unless they got the location of the cabin from Savannah. She trusted her friend not to tell.

Krista grinned as she remembered how Kye's behavior had left Savannah speechless. That didn't happen very often, and it certainly wouldn't last long.

Kye was in for a surprise if he thought he could boss Savannah around. Krista wouldn't be surprised if Savannah *did* bring out the lariat and rope him like a rowdy bull with too much testosterone.

Thoughts of Kye led to thoughts of Lyan and Adan and the ache Krista felt when she drove away from Las Vegas returned with a vengeance. She couldn't lie to herself. After the encounter with Kye, she'd been half-expecting, half-hoping that Lyan and Adan would show up.

A wave of loneliness washed over her and tears filled her eyes. God, she missed them.

Daytime. Nighttime. All the time.

The need for them never left her.

And the dreams…

Her body tightened, her nipples going to hard, aching points as her clit stiffened.

Since she'd left them her dreams had changed, become a blend of erotic and surreal. Both Adan and Lyan appeared in them, sometimes as men and sometimes as…

Krista's panties grew wet remembering how they'd loved her in her dreams, how Adan had appeared as an angel, driving his cock into her as he held her cocooned and protected in velvet-soft wings laced with gold.

And Lyan… She shivered. In her dreams he always took her to her hands and knees, biting her buttocks until she spread her legs, then laving her wet pussy and sucking on her clit until she was shaking with need and begging.

Just when she thought she couldn't take it anymore, he'd cover her, holding her wrists to the floor, pounding in and out of her as suede-soft bat-wings formed a tent around them, trapping the heat and the smell of their mating within.

Drawing in a deep, shaky breath, Krista tried to push the images from her mind. But it was too late. She was already painfully aroused.

Setting the glass of tea down on the porch railing, she braced one hand on the wood and pushed the other into her panties.

Her clit was standing at attention, throbbing with need. She moistened her fingers in her own juices then circled the swollen nub, teasing the sensitive head and the smooth underside, all the while pretending that Lyan and Adan were stroking her with their tongues, until finally the walls of her vagina spasmed, giving her a small measure of relief while leaving her more needy than ever.

Krista shuddered and pulled her hand out of her panties, afraid now that she'd been a fool to insist on leaving them. Maybe they could protect her.

But as quickly as the idea tempted her, an image of Matt strapped down to keep his bones in place, tubes running in and out of him, as doctors and nurses wandered in and out to check his condition, flashed through her mind. On its heels came the image of Alexi killing in cold blood.

No. She'd done the right thing. She'd done the only thing possible.

It wasn't just Alexi she had to worry about, but his father and uncle and the rest of his organization. If something happened to the only heir, they'd never stop until they'd had their revenge. Krista shivered, remembering Alexi's veiled warning when he'd trapped her on the yacht. His father had loved only one woman, as Alexi claimed to love Krista. All had gone well until his mother tried to abandon them. Then she'd "disappeared".

Krista shook her thoughts off and returned to the kitchen, setting the iced tea she was drinking down on the counter. It was time to hit the casinos. Wallowing in sadness and worry wasn't going to do her any good, but making money would.

Usually she was a shorts or jeans kind of person, but today Krista forced herself to change into a barely there, light blue skirt with a feminine, matching top. The whole outfit flattered her tan and made her eyes even more noticeable. Seeing herself in the mirror lifted her spirits. She only wished that Adan and Lyan were here to see it.

That thought made her laugh instead of cry. Yeah, right. This outfit would last all of two seconds before they had it ripped off her body.

Krista's entire body went taut at the image. She took a deep breath and pushed the erotic fantasy away before leaving the cabin. She needed to be with people, at least for a little while.

She pulled the car around from its parking place behind the cabin and sped off, careful to watch for any sign that might mean she'd been discovered. Several times during the last couple of days she'd stepped out of the cabin and had the vague sense of not being alone, and yet the urge to flee hadn't assailed her as it usually did when she felt watched. She'd attributed the sensation to the wildlife that lived and hid in the woods surrounding the cabin, but that didn't mean she would drop her guard.

As relaxing as the cabin was, it was somewhat of a relief to get to the row of people-filled casinos. Krista laughed at herself. Acknowledging that she was exchanging the woods for a jungle of a different type.

She exchanged real money for casino chips and headed for the blackjack tables. Every gambler has their own routine, their own set of superstitions in order to bring about good luck and success. Krista's smile was self-deprecating as she began her ritual. It was something she couldn't help, even though she knew that in the end it would be her mathematical ability along with her ability to remember the cards played, that would see her pile of chips increase rather than decrease.

Her first order of business was to play several hands of electronic poker. She never expected to win anything, but it calmed her, primed her subconscious, and helped center her. Inwardly she laughed at herself. Yeah, right.

Once she'd finished with the poker machines, she casually strolled by each of the blackjack tables, stopping for a few seconds at each in order to determine whether or not the dealer seemed friendly or hostile or mechanical.

When she'd been free of worry, she'd always chosen a mechanical dealer, one whose thoughts were elsewhere, who wouldn't distract her with emotion. Today it wouldn't matter what type of dealer worked the table she would choose. Her ultimate table selection would rest on how secure the placement was, whether she'd be able to concentrate on the game instead of watching her back. But rituals were important, so she carefully studied each dealer, and in so doing let her mind settle and prepare itself for play.

Today she was in luck. The type of dealer she preferred was stationed at the most secure table. Krista waited for a seat to open, then took her place. After that, time was meaningless.

From a distance, Adan and Lyan watched. Both felt pleasure at each of her successes.

Our mate does well, Lyan said. *Perhaps we should teach her how to play Sauris and then retire to the Kotaka Gaming Sector.*

Adan chuckled. *Our retirement would never last. How many times have we slipped into that region and extricated a lawbreaker? If we were not avoiding repercussions we would be hosting other hunters! It will be hard enough to keep the attention of other males away from our mate when we return to Belizair. Think of the challenge we would face in the Kotaka where females of such beauty are rare.*

Lyan growled. *Let any male on Belizair or elsewhere touch Krista and it will be the last female flesh he ever touches.*

Adan's eyebrows lifted. *And what of Kye? Did you not see in Krista's mind that your cousin shared a kiss with her? Should I send word to his family that he is a hunted man now?*

I will forgive him only because he kept Krista safe and she felt no lust for him. I will accept that his kiss offered only comfort. An unexpected grin flashed across Lyan's face. *I had given up hope that Kye would ever shake off the yoke of the Council. He has never been one to break the rules. This time on Earth has been good for him. It would be a shame to end his life before he had a chance to return home and act as a Vesti should.*

Adan snorted. *You mean as YOU would. How you continue to escape punishment for bending the rules time and time again, I will never understand.*

Clapping broke out at Krista's table and the men hastily turned their attention back to their mate. Her chips had tripled.

Adan grinned. *She will fit in well with our people. After she has learned our ways, I am sure she will be asked to teach. With her mathematical ability and gentle beauty, students will flock to her learning room.*

Lyan nodded. *Her transition should be smooth. I do not think her mind will rebel at our way of communicating or at the total merging that occurs when bonded mates lower their mental shields and become one in both mind and body. With her mind free of waking concerns, it was easy to reach her and know her thoughts, far easier than I had expected. On several occasions the connection deepened…*

Adan frowned. *Do you think she saw your true —*

The conversation was cut short by the arrival of three women. All three were tall, willowy, with figures that would have appealed to Adan and Lyan before they met Krista.

The redhead in the center smiled and said, "Well, hello there. Aren't you two a matched pair? My friends and I have been watching you. Would you like to join us for a drink?"

Lyan half-snarled at them, finding their perfume and nearness cloying. He shifted so that he could see Krista. She was in the process of placing a bet.

"I'm afraid we're taken," Adan said.

The girl standing in front of him frowned. "Tell me you're not gay! That would be a total waste!"

"It is a waste to be gay?" Adan said. To Lyan he sent, *I, for one, would welcome a lightening of your spirits.*

The woman in front of Lyan shifted so that her breasts rubbed against his chest, then before he could react, she shocked him by running her fingers along his cock. It was already rock-hard from being in Krista's presence.

"I don't think he prefers men," the woman said with a giggle.

Lyan growled and stepped away from her, appalled by her words, repulsed by the perfumed smell that now rose from his clothing. "I am no man-lover!" Even though it existed among the Vesti, it was not accepted or spoken of as it was among Adan's people.

Adan snickered, though only Lyan heard it. Then Adan, too, was moving back as the two women closest to him stepped forward and began to touch him.

He had never preferred to be the one pursued, though on occasion he accepted what was offered to him. But now that he had a mate-bond with Krista, he had no desire for any other.

The woman to his left giggled. "There's no need to be afraid of us. We won't hurt you...not unless you want us to."

Adan moved back further, trying to avoid the grasping hands and not call attention to himself. He could feel the blood rush to his face and prayed that none of his race were here to witness the spectacle of an Amato warrior retreating as two human females advanced on him. If word got back to his father and brothers, he would never live it down! He glanced over to find Lyan also retreating, being pushed further into the maze of machines.

Finally Adan came to a stop when he bumped into an old woman. She directed a frown at his pursuers. "Young ladies, get a hotel room! This is no place for that!" she said then turned to pull a lever.

Almost immediately a siren sounded and lights began flashing. The elderly woman screeched and hugged Adan, jumping up and down and babbling that it was his presence that changed her luck. An excited crowd began gathering and Adan saw that Lyan was also trapped in the human wave pulsing toward the slot machine.

All around him, voices were echoing the same thing, "It's Big Bob! Big Bob is finally paying out! I think he was up to a hundred and twenty million!"

Tourists pulled out cameras, pointing them at the elderly woman clutching Adan's arms. Within seconds he was trapped in white glare as cameras clicked and flashbulbs went off.

Lyan's chuckle moved through Adan's mind. *No doubt the Council will find some way to blame your fall from grace on me. It will be amusing to see you dance in front of them as I have so many times and explain how it was that you broke such an important rule as to leave no trace of yourself behind when you visited Earth.*

Adan tried to pull away from the woman but despite her frail appearance, her grip was as tight as a warrior's. "No, young man. Stay here. Please. You're my witness. You saw me pull the lever. They won't try to cheat me if they see you here."

Men in suits were quickly pushing through the crowd. Adan growled low in this throat and looked to where Lyan was now trying to extricate himself from the pressing mass of people. *You return to Krista?*

Yes. She has moved further away.

I will join you soon.

Lyan's only response was a deep chuckle that made Adan wish they were on the jungle planet, Farini, so that he could enjoy challenging Lyan to a game of Arunda, a bounty hunter training game in which the loser returned home bruised in both ego and body.

Chapter Nine

ဆ

Krista noticed the hatchet-faced man moments after a siren broke out in the casino and people began moving toward the legendary slot machine. He was standing near a doorway, talking on a cell phone. As people shifted away from him, he looked nervous. It was the nervousness that brought him to Krista's attention, that and the way his eyes darted to the exit closest to Krista, then to a second man fighting against the tide of people and heading her way. Hired muscle.

Both men fit the image of someone who'd be working for Alexi, though Krista only had to listen to her internal alarm to know that she needed to get out of the casino immediately. She scooped up her chips and made for the exit, with both men behind her, no longer bothering to hide the fact that they were in pursuit.

Out of the corner of her eye she saw Hatchet-face almost yelling into the phone. His behavior triggered a caution flag and she swerved at the last minute, avoiding the exit and trying to lose herself in the crowd. For the most part, the men hunting her had worked alone. But already she knew there were two today, and probably a third waiting outside to grab her.

Krista increased her pace until she spotted a larger group of people, visitors here for a convention probably. More women than men, most in their twenties and early thirties. She slipped in among them, smiling as though she recognized them from meetings that they were all attending. Several returned her smile.

The hired muscle passed, hurrying forward. Several minutes went by. When there was no sign of the hatchet-faced man, Krista grew uneasy, afraid that she'd let herself be trapped.

The group she'd hidden among began to splinter, drawn to different games. Krista knew that she needed to make her move soon. She was sorry now that she'd picked one of the smaller casinos. It limited the number of exits and increased the odds that she'd choose the wrong one.

Once again she looked around for the hatchet-faced man but didn't find him. The siren and excitement surrounding Big Bob had stopped. Now there was a steady flow of people spreading out, returning to their gambling. Their renewed excitement and optimism pulsed through the casino, each thinking that today would be the day they hit the jackpot, too, and Krista felt buoyed by their hope.

She backtracked to the exit she'd originally intended to leave by. The odds suggested that her pursuers would have continued forward, thinking to get ahead of her.

There was no sign of the hatched-faced man or the hired muscle as Krista moved to join a small group of people and left the casino with them. Once outside, she headed for her car, merging continuously with clusters of people as she tried to hurry yet remain unnoticed.

Within a block she knew that she was being followed. Her instincts screamed for her to run and she didn't try to argue with them.

As she ran, she cursed herself for wandering so far from the car and for giving in to the temptation to wear such a feminine outfit. The delicate sandals weren't as easy to run in as her usual tennis shoes.

She was almost to the lot where her car was parked when the hatchet-faced man suddenly stepped out from behind a van, the phone still pressed to his ear. His face wore a triumphant expression.

Krista's heart pounded in her ears, her breath was already laboring in and out from running in the Reno heat. She turned, ready to dart across the street, but saw the hired muscle rapidly approaching. There was no doubt in her mind that a third man was somewhere behind her. She turned anyway, knowing that being among people was her best shot of escaping capture.

The third man was impossible to miss. He was moving in on her fast, sweat dripping off his heavy body, his round face flushed from the heat and exercise. Of the three, he was her best bet, the weakest link, maybe.

Krista rushed toward him, knowing that she'd only have one shot at getting past him and out of the parking lot. Praying that the men weren't smart enough to think of tranquilizer darts, or that Alexi hadn't decided that he'd be just as happy to know she was dead.

The third man grinned as she moved toward him. Krista waited until the last minute then changed directions. In the split second it took him to redirect his heavy body, she made it around him, only to see that the hired muscle was quickly overtaking her.

She opened her mouth to scream, not wanting to wait until it was too late. But before the first hint of sound could escape, Lyan and Adan stormed into sight, their expressions fierce and deadly.

Krista raced toward them, relief warring with fear. Uncertain whether to throw herself at them, or move past, accepting their help without exposing them to additional danger.

Adan didn't give her a choice. As soon as she was close, he grabbed her, hugging her to him briefly before pushing her into Lyan's uncompromising grasp.

Krista saw that the three men had retreated, but not disappeared. The hatchet-faced man was on his phone. She shivered, wondering if he was calling Alexi.

"Please, let's leave now," Krista said.

Adan laughed. "I will deal with them while Lyan gets you to safety."

"No, Adan, please. Just leave it. Don't get involved any further," Krista pleaded.

He turned to her and his face softened as he brushed his lips against hers. "Do not beg for something I cannot give you. Go with Lyan now so that I do not have to worry about your safety."

To Lyan he added, *The fever rides you hard, my friend. While I get my satisfaction in battle, you can find yours as you try to tame our mate.*

Try? Lyan answered, his voice holding all the arrogance of a Vesti male.

Adan chuckled. *I will join you in the cabin after I have sent a warning and a challenge to the man who terrorizes Krista.*

Good. I would have justice done on her behalf before we leave this primitive planet.

Lyan escorted Krista to her car, then eased her into the passenger seat and saw her safely buckled in before getting in the driver's seat and starting the engine. There was a moment's satisfaction as the vehicle moved forward. Primitive, yet strangely pleasant. He would tinker with these transport devices if he were forced to stay on this planet for a long period of time.

The three men had scattered as soon as they saw her leaving and Adan approaching. Now there was no sign of any of them.

Krista turned away from her window and glared at Lyan. Adrenaline and fear were still raging through her body. "You followed me!"

"Of course. You belong to us. You are our bond-mate, ours to protect and pleasure. Ours to breed. Ours! Did you think we would let you go?"

His words poured over her like lava. "Ours to breed!"

Lyan's nostrils flared. His cock pressed against the front of his jeans. "Yes."

Her womb fluttered at his words. Her nipples tightened. She wanted to dive into the fantasy they created and never emerge. But her survival instinct protested.

"I don't think so," she said.

Lyan's hands tightened on the steering wheel. He didn't respond. He was no master with words. His body would show her the truth.

Let her challenge him! The surrender would only be that much sweeter.

They drove the rest of the way to the cabin in silence. He took only enough time to make sure that all was secure, then he ushered her inside.

As soon as he closed the front door, Lyan unbuttoned his shirt and shrugged out of it. "Take your clothes off. I have need of my mate. It has been too many days since my cock tunneled into your welcoming sheath. Strip or I will shred your clothing."

Krista gasped. Torn between outrage, amusement, and lust. Her mind struggled to find a suitable comeback. She had to settle on a simple word. "No."

Lyan's hands moved to his jeans and whipped them off. "It was foolish to let you drive off. It was foolish to let you separate from us. You were made for us. For me. Strip, Krista. Now. Or I will punish you."

Heat surged through her, a fire she didn't recognize in herself. This love-play was beyond anything she'd ever experienced before.

She stared at Lyan's fully engorged cock. "You don't own me," she challenged, watching the effect her words had on him.

His cock jerked and grew even larger. A low growl rumbled through his chest. He moved toward her, his strong, dark hand circling his shaft, pumping once, then again.

An unknown excitement rushed through Krista. He was male animal. Primitive man.

She moved away, circling the sofa. His eyes sharpened with anticipation. "Before this day is over, you will agree to go through the binding ceremony. Before this day is over, I will have you in every way a male can take his female," Lyan told her.

Krista shuddered, her nipples tightening painfully at his words.

"You will know who is master of your body by the time we are done," he promised in a husky whisper. "You will need my cock as you need to breathe. You will plead to go through the binding ceremony and return home with us."

She laughed at his arrogance. "You'll be the one begging," she shot back, white-hot desire tracing along her spine as her panties became soaked.

A sensual smile slipped across his masculine features. Seconds later he lunged at her, but instinct honed from months of being on the run kicked in. She evaded him, though at the cost of her shirt. It ripped from her body as if it were made of paper.

Lyan growled, his eyes dilating as the remains of her shirt fluttered to the carpet. "Surrender now and I won't punish you."

Krista moved around a chair, closer to the door that led to her bedroom. She'd have to be very fast to get through it and close it before Lyan reached her.

"I'm not the type to give up," she told him.

He shrugged, his eyes never leaving her face. The full-heat of the Vesti mating fever was on him now. It ripped through his body demanding the total submission of his mate. Perhaps if Adan were here... Lyan did not bother to explore the thought further. There was nothing to stop him from giving in to his instinct. From binding her to him in the way of his people.

Krista tensed as though she would run for the front door, but Lyan knew what her true intentions were. The moment she bolted, he was on her, swooping her up and moving into the bedroom, her struggles only adding to his excitement.

She expected him to toss her on the mattress and drive his thick cock into her. Instead he sat on the edge of the bed and flipped her over so that she lay across his lap. With one hand he quickly stripped her of her remaining clothes.

"Accept that you belong to us. That you are our bond-mate, ours to protect and pleasure, ours to breed, and I will let you escape your punishment," he said as his hand moved over her bare ass in a possessive caress.

"No."

He raised his hand and brought it down on her naked buttocks. Krista's heart pounded in her ears. The small pain shocked her, but the arousal stunned her.

Even in her wildest fantasies she'd never considered punishment like this erotic. But as his palm smoothed over her tingling skin before slapping her again, she couldn't deny that it was turning her on.

She fought against his hold on her. She fought the arousal. But the fighting only seemed to drive it higher and higher. Her inner thighs were wet, her labia engorged and her nipples tight and sensitive.

"Please, Lyan," she finally cried, feeling his cock burning against her side and needing it inside her so badly that she was willing to beg for it.

He eased her off his lap so that she was on her knees in front of him. His face was a feral mask, his eyes completely black with desire.

"Suck my cock as a true mate would," he demanded. The words, the dominance, made her pussy clench. There was no thought to disobey him, but the spanking had not reduced her to submission. If anything, it made her want to test her own feminine power.

Krista's hands rested against his rock-hard thighs. She leaned forward and watched in satisfaction as his washboard stomach tightened. His breath caught in his throat when her lips hovered over the huge purple head of his penis. He groaned when her tongue slowly washed over the engorged head, before moving to explore the rest of his shaft, but she did not take him into the warmth of her mouth as he had commanded.

Lyan grabbed her head. "Suck my cock, Krista, now!" he demanded.

She laughed softly, her hands moving so that one could circle his shaft while the other explored his tight, heavy balls.

He bucked against her, groaning, and struggled to control himself. Krista tightened her hold on his shaft as she cupped and stroked his balls, touching his tip with her lips and teasing him with the slick surface of her tongue. His hands fisted in her hair, holding her still so that he could push his cock in and out of her mouth.

The sensations were beyond anything Lyan had ever experienced, had ever imagined. Every drop of blood, every nerve ending felt as though it belonged to his cock. He was in agony and only Krista could provide him with relief.

His heart pounded, filled with love, desire, excitement such as he had never known, as he pumped in and out of her hot mouth.

"Krista!" he shouted.

His need was a powerful aphrodisiac. Her hand moved up his shaft, making it impossible for him to shove more than his engorged tip into her mouth.

He growled and Krista began sucking him, slowly at first, then harder.

Lyan's grip in her hair tightened and he arched his back. His face was a study in exquisite need, of fierce masculinity.

Krista opened her mouth wider, wanting to swallow him whole. Wanting to suck him into her very being.

Lyan groaned as Krista took him all the way to the back of her throat, sucking him as though she would take everything from him, moaning when he pulled away, only to take more of him in on the next stroke.

His balls tightened. There was no holding back now. Fingers of pleasure were shooting through his testicles and cock, urging him to thrust faster, harder.

He came in an endless wave of ecstasy. And knew a primitive satisfaction when Krista swallowed all of his seed.

Lyan shuddered and panted with the pleasure she had given him. His cock surged to life again when she nuzzled against the inside of his thigh, taking his skin between her teeth and marking him as hers.

With a low growl he took her to the soft carpet, turning her so that she was on her hands and knees before him.

Unerringly his mouth went to the mark on her neck and his mating fangs sank into the tender flesh. She groaned and arched against him, the smell of her arousal flooding his senses.

Her smooth thighs yielded as he used his own to push them apart. She was soaking in desire. Lyan groaned as his cock encountered her wet heat.

There was no thought, only the burning need to be inside her. Lyan plunged his full length into her, then began pounding in and out, mindless to anything but the extreme pleasure. Krista writhed beneath him, inflaming him further, making the need to dominate spin out of control.

Lyan thought he would die from the pleasure of mating with her. Her hot sheath clung to his cock, tight and wet and welcoming. With each plunge inward he felt his balls touch her swollen flesh. He'd never felt so powerful, so possessive and yet so possessed.

"Come for me," he ordered, only to demand it again and again after she'd obeyed him.

Even after Lyan had finally allowed himself release, he didn't pull out of Krista's welcoming body. He held her tightly and shifted just enough so that he wasn't crushing her. The mating fever had lessened its grip on him, but he was not finished yet.

The muscles along his back quivered and he ached to let her see all of him, to let the protection that the Ylan crystal provided drop, so that he could wrap his wings around her, trapping the heat and the scent of their lovemaking around them. But she was not yet bound to them and his heart would splinter like Sarien glass if she recoiled in horror.

Of its own accord, his hand traveled along her flat stomach and down to the soft golden hair between her thighs. He cupped her pussy possessively and pressed his palm against her clit. Krista whimpered, so sensitized that his touch bordered on pain. "Consider me punished and surrendered. I don't think I can go another round."

Lyan smiled against her silky hair. "So you agree to go through the binding ceremony and return home with us?"

"Let's not argue," she pleaded. "If anything, today should prove how dangerous it is to be seen with me."

"If anything, today should prove to you that our vow of protection can be relied on. Even now Adan deals with those that would take you from us."

Krista shivered and snuggled back against his chest. "Don't you think you should go check on him?"

Lyan's entire body shook with his laughter. "Adan would be insulted if I thought he couldn't handle those three Earth...eaters."

"Earth eaters?"

Lyan chuckled. "I'm sorry. I became carried away with visions of going to Adan's aid. Those men are pathetic, hardly worth Adan's effort. But should I interfere with his fun, he would challenge me to a fight instead."

"Men!" Krista grumbled.

"More than just men," Lyan said. "Your mates. Mates who will no longer allow you to put yourself in danger."

Fire flashed in Krista's eyes and she stiffened in his arms. "And I don't have anything to say about it?"

Lyan's eyes narrowed and his nostrils flared as the mating fever rose within him. His cock was rock-hard as he pulled it out of her. She whimpered, her body following his, trying to keep them joined, already knowing and accepting what it needed to survive.

Without a word he got up and went to the living room, scooping his jeans up off the floor and taking a small tube out of the pocket before letting the pants fall to the carpet once again. When he returned to the bedroom, he found Krista sitting in the middle of the bed.

Lyan crawled onto the bed, using the sheer size of his body to force her onto her back. Krista wrapped her legs around his hips, her eyes flashing with defiance, with her resolve not to be sexually dominated.

The part of Lyan's mind controlled by the mating fever saw her challenge and leaped to accept it. He slipped the tube containing a special lubricant under the pillow, then took Krista's wrists in his hands and held them to the mattress above her head.

"You belong to me. For now. Forever. Say you will go through the binding ceremony."

She rubbed against him, making him shudder as her slick juices coated his cock. "Let's just enjoy this moment in time, Lyan," she whispered in response. "Make love to me again. I need your body in mine."

Lyan's body gave an involuntary thrust, seating him in her hot depths before he could stop himself. Krista pressed her lips against his neck, her body arching into his, wanting to swallow his up in victory.

"No," Lyan growled, pulling out of her and flipping her onto her stomach. "Give me what I want, Krista," he demanded as he brought his body down on hers. "Agree to a permanent bond."

She pressed against him enticingly. "When it's safe. If you still want it. Please, Lyan. Let's not argue. Make love to me."

Lyan's body throbbed with demand, with the need to lose himself in her wet, hot depths. But his soul, his heart refused to let his cock rule this time.

He shifted his hands so that only one was needed to hold her wrists to the bed. With his free hand, he retrieved the tube of lubricant. His lips curled in a silent snarl as he remembered the Council worker who'd been forced to come up with a design that would not arouse suspicion yet would not yield the secret of its contents should it be left on Earth. Curse the Council and all their rules. What harm would come to the humans if they discovered and found a way to duplicate the ritzca oil of the Vesti? Was it not already a favored import across the universe?

Lyan eased off of Krista far enough so that he could run a finger along the cleft of her ass. Her breath caught in her throat and she tried to move away from his hand.

He laughed and threw a dark, muscled leg over hers, making it impossible for her to escape his touch. She shivered when his fingers separated her ass cheeks and zeroed in on the puckered skin surrounding her anus.

"I will have you here next, Krista," he said as he squeezed the tube of lubricant in his palm and watched several drops slide down his fingers and onto Krista. She arched as the heated oil immediately went to work, coating her tissue and making her even more aware of each nerve ending.

Lyan's cock twitched and a drop of pre-cum glistened on its velvet tip. The oil would heat her skin, heighten the need, yet at the same time lubricate her so that the pain of his penetration would blend into unbelievable pleasure for both of them.

He rubbed the oil in, dipping one finger into the tempting hole in front of him. Krista whimpered and tried to escape his touch. Her response told him that she'd never been breached in this manner before. It sent more blood to his nearly bursting cock. The thought of being the first to have her in this way almost made him spew his seed across the creamy globes of her ass.

Lyan pressed his face against her neck. "It does no good to fight the bond between us," he said in a husky voice as he sent more of the lubricant down his fingers and into her anus. "You will scream in pleasure and beg for more. You belong only to us, just as we belong only to you."

Krista bucked against him, causing his finger to move deeper into the tight canal.

Lyan groaned and added a second finger to the first. "Imagine what it will be like to have both Adan and I inside you at once, filling your pussy and your ass. Joining with you and making the three of us one entity, one connected being. That is the way we have chosen to perform the binding ceremony." He nuzzled her neck and sent more lubricant into her quivering opening. "Tell me you do not want to join that way, Krista. Tell me that you do not want to mate with us in that manner."

Krista whimpered and arched against his hand. Her body was covered in a light layer of sweat, as was his.

Lyan filled her with even more of the ritzca oil then moved so that his leg was no longer trapping her lower body to the bed. Krista shivered and pulled her knees under her, positioning herself so that he could easily slip into the part of her that now screamed for his possession.

"Please, Lyan. Please."

Lyan's hips bucked involuntarily at the sight in front of him. His mate spread for his pleasure. Submissive to him. The mating fever of the Vesti roared through him as he moved to cover Krista's body with his.

Chapter Ten

ஐ

Krista shivered. Every nerve in her body felt stretched tight with anticipation as Lyan moved. The heat rolling off his body and onto hers echoed the fiery ache centered in her anus. But when she felt the velvet head of his penis pressed against her unexplored opening she was torn between moving into him and moving away from him.

His lips whispered across her neck and shoulders. "Easy, beloved," he said, his voice gentle despite his dominating position.

"Lyan." It came out a soft, needy sound, submissive.

He groaned and surged against her, moving so that just the very tip of him was inside her.

Krista tightened around him, in protest, in confused demand, the pain melting into pleasure.

Lyan growled, moving out, then pressing further into her as one hand slid around and began stroking and pumping her clit.

Krista was overwhelmed by sensation. With a sob she spread herself wider, offered more of herself. "Please," she whimpered, but Lyan did not give in to her plea.

His fingers slowed and Krista almost came when he rubbed the first drop of heated lubricant onto her stiff, erect clit. It felt as if every nerve ending in her body was centered in her clit and ass.

She buried her face against the mattress, afraid that she'd agree to anything he wanted as his oil-slick fingers moved down her engorged clit and into her already aching vagina.

He stroked in and out, using both his cock and his fingers to drive the pleasure higher. "This is a weak imitation of what it will be like when Adan and I both possess you at the same time," Lyan said against her neck, against the place where he'd bitten her. "Agree to the binding ceremony," he urged, rubbing his palm against her pulsing clit as he pushed into her deeply with his fingers and cock.

Krista screamed and bucked against him, caught on the edge of a powerful orgasm, desperate to go over.

Lyan pulled back and Krista whimpered.

"Agree and I will give you the release you seek," Lyan said as he gently bit down on her neck.

Krista shivered, her emotions and body rioting, convinced that she needed this in order to survive. "Yes," she sobbed and Lyan's victorious growl filled the room as he let go of his control and drove Krista to an orgasm so exquisite that it sent her into oblivion.

When she woke, she was nuzzling a bare chest. Adan.

Krista pressed a soft kiss against his smooth skin and was rewarded by a hug. "So you are finally awake."

She licked the small brown nipple, then sucked it lightly before moving back a few inches so that she could take in his naked body. There didn't seem to be a single bruise or scratch on it. Still, she couldn't stop herself from asking, "You're okay?"

Adan's teeth flashed in a superior masculine smile. "Of course. You do not need to worry that they will try for you again. I was able to persuade them that if they continued in Alexi's service, they would suffer his same fate."

Krista stiffened at the mention of Alexi's name. "You talked to them about Alexi?"

"Yes. But as a gift to my bond-mate, I spared their lives — this first time." He shrugged. "If they are so stupid as to attempt to take you again, then they will die. Just as Alexi will die if he doesn't heed the warning I sent to him."

Krista's heart raced in the confines of her chest. This was exactly what she didn't want to happen! "Does Alexi know who you are?"

"My name?"

Krista felt like screaming, but took a deep breath instead. Men! The more danger, the more testosterone! "Yes."

Adan shrugged. "The men he sent know of Lyan and me. Whether our names were spoken in their presence or not is unimportant. What is important is that they know you are no longer alone, unprotected and unclaimed, and they have passed this knowledge on to the one you have feared. It is enough. You are safe now."

Irritation flashed through Krista. Neither Adan nor Lyan had listened to a word she said. They thought a show of muscle and a threat of violence would scare Alexi off. They didn't accept that *she* knew him a lot better! Knew that *nothing* would deter him.

"I've got to move on. He's probably already got people looking around Reno for me. It won't be long before they find someone who knows where I am, or that I used to come here with my parents," she said, not bothering to hide her anger. Adan's eyes narrowed but he didn't stop her when she got out of bed and went into the bathroom.

Krista climbed into the shower, trying to calm herself with hot water and a few minutes without either Adan or Lyan nearby. Her emotions assaulted her, a maelstrom that she didn't have any control of. They'd reduced her to this!

She took a deep breath and closed her eyes. Of their own accord, memories of Lyan's domination flooded her senses. She hoped that his absence meant he was outside, guarding the cabin, because she knew it would be found. There was no "if", only "when".

Yet despite the worry, the turmoil of emotions that plagued her, Krista could feel the demand already building in her body, like a separate pulse, the name Adan sounding with every heartbeat. Her body clamoring for his touch with the same desperation it had felt for Lyan's. Whatever the two of them had done to her, she was like an addict now.

Krista turned so that she was leaning against wall as the hot water struck her back. The quiet click of the shower opening and closing told her that Adan had joined her.

"Lyan said that you agreed to go through the binding ceremony."

Krista shivered as the image of Adan and Lyan taking her at the same time filled her with aching need. "I did. I will. It doesn't change the fact that we need to get out of here."

"You do not trust us," Adan said against the soft skin at her nape.

"It's not about trusting you! It's about not wanting anything to happen to you. Do you have any idea how horrible I would feel!" Just the idea made tears rush to her eyes.

Adan forced her to turn. He stroked her hair then cupped her face, holding it still while his lips whispered a kiss across hers. "It is time you learned to trust," he said leading her from the shower and smoothing her body dry with a towel, before drying himself.

Krista reached for her clothing, but Adan stopped her by grabbing both of her wrists. "No."

Her body reacted with a sensual shiver. "No?"

"It is time you learned to trust," he repeated. There was firm resolve in his usually tender face as he led her through the bedroom and out to the kitchen.

Adan took a seat at the table and pulled her onto his lap. She could feel his half-aroused cock pressed against her naked buttocks.

Sunshine poured through the windows and Krista realized she didn't have any idea what time it was. Her stomach growled when she caught sight of the sliced oranges and bananas arranged on a plate in the middle of the table. But when she reached for a slice of fruit, Adan once again grabbed her wrist. "No. I will feed you."

Krista laughed and tried to pull out of his grip. He responded by shifting so that both of her wrists were locked in front of her by one of his hands. Then he casually reached toward the fruit. "Would you prefer some banana or some orange?"

"I can feed myself."

Adan brushed his lips across her neck and shoulder. "A bite of banana or a slice of orange?"

She turned so that she could meet his eyes. "I'd rather feed myself."

He reached for a slice of orange and popped it in his mouth, chewing it slowly, then swallowing as Krista watched. When he was done, he pressed his lips to hers and slowly invaded her mouth with his tongue. The sweet flavor of orange made her stomach clinch in protest. "Banana or orange?" he asked again.

"Banana."

He reached for a slice of banana and offered it to her. She took it from his fingers, careful not to touch his skin, to further acknowledge what he was trying to do to her.

Adan laughed softly. "Another?"

She nodded but instead of feeding her immediately, Adan trailed kisses down her neck and over her collarbone. When she whimpered, he reached for another piece of banana and offered it to her. Of its own accord, her tongue stroked over his fingers as she took the piece of fruit.

Adan smiled and repeated the process over and over again until Krista willingly took whatever he offered. By the time he carried her to bed, her arousal swamped his senses and burned though his blood just as her acceptance of him was a fire in his heart and soul.

Krista's need was so intense that she arched toward Adan as soon as she felt the cool sheet touch her back. She was so wet and swollen she ached.

He lay down next to her, shifting so that one leg held her lower body in place while his hands shackled her wrists and raised them above her head. In a split second, before the sensual haze could dissipate and reality set in, he'd spread her arms and bound her hands to the headboard.

Krista came back to earth in a rush. "You don't need to tie me up to make love to me."

Adan pressed his chest against hers, held her down with his weight. "Not to make love to you, but to continue your lesson on trust."

"I trust you. Let me go so I can touch you."

"Not yet," he said, then eased down her body, kissing her softly as he went. This time he didn't catch her by surprise, but the outcome wasn't changed regardless. Her legs were spread, held open by ankles tied to the bedposts.

"Adan," she pleaded, not exactly sure what she wanted.

His eyes were dark with arousal now. He began kissing his way back up her body. The kisses were firm, possessive. When he reached the inside of her thigh he bit down, marking her on either side of her dripping pussy.

"Adan," she said again. Arching, offering herself, begging.

His tongue dipped into her slit in a quick probe. "You do not know how long I have waited for a mate, dreamed of a mate." He thrust again and she whimpered. "To have a mate such as you is beyond my wildest fantasies."

This time he licked from the base of her slit up and over her clit. Krista jerked against the ties keeping her from wrapping her body around his.

Adan's fingers pinched and pulled on her nipples as he took her clit into his mouth and began suckling. Krista struggled against the orgasm, but the sensations crashing into her were overwhelming, intense, and she couldn't hold out against them. She screamed and shuddered in release and Adan pressed his face into her sopping wet cunt and began licking up her juices, groaning as though he would make a meal of her. It sent Krista over again, gave her an orgasm that had her sobbing for his cock to pierce her.

When he pulled away, he was breathing hard. "Make love to me," Krista pleaded.

"Not yet." Adan leaned forward and began kissing her stomach, biting down gently then soothing the spot with his tongue. "I can hardly wait to take you home and plant my seed in your womb, to see you swell with our children."

Krista's vagina pulsed. Her womb ached. Her nipples were so tight they hurt.

Adan kissed his way upward, stopping only to leave a mark over her heart, before trailing his tongue back and forth over her nipple.

Krista arched and sobbed, "Please, Adan," and he responded by taking the nipple into his mouth and gently suckling while his penis rubbed along her slit, bathing in its wetness. He moved to the other nipple, first suckling gently, then harder, sending wave after wave of pleasure and need right to her womb.

"Please," she whimpered again.

Adan's lips abandoned her nipple, but his fingers took over the steady stimulation as he kissed his way up until his face hovered only inches above hers. Desire burned, a hot flame in his eyes, a thin layer of sweat on his fully aroused body. "This is what the thought of mating with you does to me." He lowered his head and sucked a nipple as though he wanted to swallow it. When he finally released it, he said, "I want to see our sons nursing at your breasts. I want to know that you truly accept the pleasure and protection of your mates. That you trust us to take care of you." He pressed just the head of his penis into her slit. His eyes stared into hers as he gently took a nipple in his mouth and sucked.

Krista arched and sobbed, wanting what he wanted, wanting to yield everything to him.

He released the nipple and moved to the other one, taking it in his mouth and sucking gently, as though he worshipped at her breast.

Something inside her gave. She wanted them. She loved them. Through the good as well as the bad.

"I trust you to take care of me," she whispered.

"You must agree to go home with us before we can complete the binding ceremony," Adan said.

"I'll go home with you."

Adan reached up and entwined his fingers with hers. "You are our hope, our future, Krista, our everything," he said before filling her with himself and making love to her over and over again.

Chapter Eleven

ဢ

Krista sat up in bed and stretched. Morning sun bathed the bedroom in gentle light. She couldn't keep the smile off of her face as she looked at Adan and Lyan. Even asleep they made her heart pound and her body tighten with desire. How in the world had she ended up with these two men?

Fear tried to intrude on her happiness, but she pushed it away. She had promised them both that she would trust them to care for her—not that she was going to drop her guard or act like some helpless female—but she would trust that they understood the risk and accepted the "worse" that came with the "better".

She slipped out of bed, laughing softly with smug satisfaction when Adan frowned and Lyan grumbled, but neither woke up. She'd worn her oh-so dominant mates out!

Heat pulsed through her at the remembered pleasure. Who'd have guessed that being dominated could be such a turn-on!

A small smile played across her lips as she thought about turning the tables on them. Not that she'd want to do it all the time, but it would be fun to tie them down one at a time and see just how aroused she could make them. Of course, she'd have to get extra strong bindings before she attempted it, especially for Lyan.

Desire hummed through her as the idea took hold and she mentally ran through what she had in the cabin that might work as restraints. She couldn't think of anything other than the ties Adan had used on her. Maybe they'd be strong enough, especially for him. Of the two, he was the gentler, the more playful. He'd probably agree to play her game.

Krista laughed. Between the two of them, they'd turned her into a sex maniac!

Quietly she made her way to the kitchen, grabbing Adan's shirt off the table and putting it on. She fixed a cup of coffee, then stepped out onto the porch. The air was warm and sweet-smelling, the view of the surrounding woods tranquil. Krista inhaled deeply, as though her very soul was absorbing the peace surrounding her.

Thoughts of wild sex gave way to questions about the binding ceremony. She felt "married" to them both already.

She frowned, thinking back to the words they'd used. Not marriage but a binding ceremony. Not husbands and wife, but a mate-bond.

The way they spoke made her think that they'd been raised in a different culture, and yet they didn't seem completely foreign. There was almost an "old-world" feel to them, as though they were raised apart from society.

Unease trickled through her. They wanted to take her to their home, and yet she had no idea where home was. They'd both said that once the binding was complete they would be tied together permanently. The way they'd said it made her believe them, made her feel as though it was the most natural thing in the world to have two husbands...that it was completely legal, and yet it wasn't.

Her thoughts fluttered briefly to her encounter with Kye. Was it possible that they lived in a tightly knit community where it was acceptable to have more than one husband...or wife? Krista's heartbeat jumped as she considered the possibility of actually sharing a life with two men, of starting a family with them.

They'd both said they wanted children, made her feel aroused just at the thought of producing those children. How many men wanted children so deeply, actually talked about mating, about planting their seed in a womb and imagining their sons nursing?

A shiver passed through Krista as reality intruded on her fantasy. What if they were members of some cult? Coming out only to secure a woman to have their children?

She looked down at the bracelets that now adorned her wrists. During the night Adan and Lyan had each clasped a bracelet on her wrist, claiming once again that she was their bond-mate.

Krista studied the intricate patterns on the two bracelets. They were identical to the patterns on the bracelets Adan and Lyan wore, though her bracelets were free of the stones that adorned theirs. She shivered again when she could find no clasp that would allow her to remove either bracelet from her wrist.

In the deepest part of her being, Krista believed that Adan and Lyan would never harm her, but if she went home with them, would she disappear, never to be seen again? Was that the price she'd have to pay, not only to be with them, but to be safe from Alexi? Was she willing to pay it? And how could she see that justice was done for the murdered policeman if she disappeared?

Krista felt panic start to grip her. She clamped down on her emotions and left the porch, deciding that a short walk would help calm her down.

Nothing was done yet. There was time for her to ask questions. She'd said that she trusted them, and she did trust them. They wouldn't take her against her will. But what if they gave her the answers she feared? Or worse, refused to answer her questions at all?

By the time she got to the edge of the woods, her instincts were screaming for her to run. Krista didn't give in to them. Instead she turned back toward the cabin, deciding to wake Adan and Lyan up when she got there.

But before she could take the first step, she was grabbed from behind and the cold barrel of a gun pressed against her temple. In that second she realized the true source of her panic.

* * * * *

Lyan woke with a start, immediately sure of two things—that Krista wasn't in the cabin and that something was wrong. He scrambled to his feet and reached for his clothing.

Adan woke instantly, coming awake fully alert. *Can you sense her?* he asked.

There was no inflection in Adan's words but Lyan could feel the pain simmering underneath the surface of them. He reached out to Krista, using the bond forged and deepened during the Vesti mating fever. His heart raced and pounded painfully in his chest when he touched her mind only to find fear masked by a cloying darkness.

She has been taken! Lyan said.

On the other side of the bed, Adan motioned toward the back of the cabin. *Someone approaches.*

Lyan barely restrained a derisive snort. *I sense only two of them.*

Adan shrugged. *Perhaps there are others waiting in the woods to see how these two fare.*

Perhaps. But we have no time to toy with them. Even now Krista moves further away from us.

Adan nodded. *They have been warned. Let us kill them and go reclaim our mate.*

Lyan's smile was feral, though amusement lurked in his eyes. *No doubt we will be called before the Council in order to justify our actions—an experience I am quite familiar with but one you have always avoided.*

So be it, Adan said seconds before sunlight bounced off the metal of a gun's barrel as it suddenly appeared in the bedroom window.

With instincts honed to perfection, Adan and Lyan both used the crystals in their wristbands against their shared enemy.

The gunman never knew what hit him. Nor did the second gunman or the two who waited just beyond the border of trees.

Chapter Twelve

ॐ

Krista woke to a pounding headache and queasy stomach. Automatically her hand moved to the knot on her temple and pain exploded in her head. She dropped her hand and saw that her fingers were coated in a thin layer of blood.

She struggled to make sense of what was happening to her, then remembered. She'd tried to fight her assailant, tried to scream out a warning to Lyan and Adan, but a second man had stepped forward and struck her with his gun. She'd lost consciousness after that.

Fear rushed in, making the nausea more difficult to manage. Krista took a deep breath and forced herself to study her surroundings, to orient herself. Where there was life, there was hope.

She was in a small bedroom with walls of cheap paneling and a tiny window covered by a gauzy curtain. The slight rocking motion drew her attention to the sound of tires traveling over asphalt.

Adan's shirt still covered her body. Krista lifted it, pressing it against her face, breathing in his scent and taking comfort from it.

Somehow, some way, she'd escape again.

Krista got to her feet, fighting dizziness and nausea as she moved unsteadily to the window. She braced her hand against the fake wood and watched as tree after tree appeared then disappeared from view. There were no street signs, no houses, no indication that anyone else existed here besides whoever was driving…and her.

She was in a motor home of some sort. She closed her eyes and leaned against the wall as she waited for the nausea to fade. When it did, she looked back out the window, recognizing the landscape this time, though not an exact location. They were in California now, near Tahoe, but far away from the vacationers and gamblers.

Krista's throat tightened. She'd never been here with Alexi, but she knew that his father and uncles had a remote hunting cabin here. A place where it would be easy to keep someone prisoner — or kill them. Her heart rate accelerated.

She forced air into her lungs and rubbed a hand across her temple, careful to skirt the lump, as she tried to clear the panic away. "Think," she whispered out loud. "Calm down and think."

Once again she pressed Adan's shirt to her face. Her heart lurched. Fear for them flooded though her. Tears rushed to her eyes as she remembered Lyan and Adan as she'd last seen them, sprawled across the bed, asleep.

What if…

Krista's throat burned. Her heart contracted into an agonized knot in her chest. For several seconds the pain was unbearable. She gasped, her fingers holding onto the cheap gauzy curtains in order to keep herself from sinking to the floor in defeat.

One sob forced itself out before the instincts that had kept her alive surged to the surface of her consciousness. She had to escape. She had to believe that Adan and Lyan were safe. There was no other choice.

Taking a deep breath, Krista drew air into her lungs and pushed the pain and fear away, out of her thoughts. There was only room for one thing now — escape, survival.

She took a step back from the window and studied its dimensions. Even if she could somehow open it without the driver seeing her through the side view mirror, the window was too small for her to climb through and the vehicle was moving fast enough that jumping would be more dangerous than taking her chances by staying.

Krista moved from the window. She was not surprised to find that the door leading into the rest of the motor home was locked.

Adan's shirt brushed against her thighs, reminding her that she was barefoot and without adequate clothing. But a quick search of the room yielded nothing of use—either to cover or to protect herself with.

The motor home began slowing, Krista went back to the window. Her heart nearly stopped when she spotted a black Mercedes parked next to a gated road. Even as she watched, the driver's door opened and a heavily muscled man climbed out of the sleek automobile. Krista recognized him immediately—Alexi's driver, Ruben. She'd tried on several occasions to make conversation with him. Each time he'd stood immobile, as though she wasn't even there. When she'd mentioned it to Alexi he'd smiled and said, "Ruben has been with me a long time. He knows what's expected of him."

Self-directed anger flashed through her. *How could I have been so stupid to just go along with things? So naïve?*

The voice of reason soothed. *Because Alexi was charming and a man like him was totally outside your experience.*

Alexi's driver opened the gate so the motor home could pass without stopping. Krista's heart pounded in her ears as they lumbered down a narrow road with tight curves and dense, dark forest on either side. There was no doubt in her mind that Alexi was waiting for her. There was also no hope that she'd be able to take them by surprise and escape. Somehow she'd have to survive and plan, just as she'd done on his yacht until a chance to get away presented itself.

Finally the cabin came into sight. It was small, especially when compared to Alexi's San Francisco home.

The motor home shuddered to a stop, its engine suddenly quiet. Krista heard the motor home's door slamming shut.

The black Mercedes pulled up next to Krista's window. Alexi's driver got out and disappeared around the front of the motor home. There was the mumble of voices and Krista was momentarily distracted from watching the cabin as she tried to hear what was being said.

When she looked again, a second of pure fear exploded in her chest. Alexi had stepped out onto the porch and was now moving toward the motor home. A satisfied smile hovered on his face though even from a distance Krista could see his hard eyes. She shuddered, remembering how they'd once seemed only warm and soft, full of tenderness and admiration.

"Bring her out," Alexi called to Ruben and the other man.

A door opened and the motor home rocked slightly as heavy footsteps made their way down the hallway, only to stop outside of the room where Krista was confined.

She inhaled deeply, forcing herself to appear calm, unafraid. Her time as a prisoner on Alexi's yacht had taught her that emotional strength and quiet confidence were a requirement of survival.

The stakes would be even higher now. Alexi would be angry at her defection. But as long as he believed there was a chance to possess her completely, he wouldn't kill her. At least not right away.

She stepped back from the door as a deadbolt slid out of place a second before the cheap wooden door was pushed forward with more force than was necessary.

Alexi's driver stood, arms slightly away from his side as though he was prepared to be assaulted—or to attack if necessary. His dark, designer clothing did not hide the bulk of his arms or the thickness of his neck.

Ruben's voice was a deep, no-nonsense rumble. "Out."

He stepped back to allow her to pass. Krista moved into the hallway. A man she didn't recognize stood at the end of hall, blocking her from any attempt toward the driver's seat.

A bubble of laughter threatened to erupt from her. *Like there was any chance she'd be able to get away from Alexi's driver, start the engine and somehow get the two men out of the motor home while she made her escape.*

Alexi was waiting as she stepped out of the motor home. His triumphant smile faded and his eyes narrowed to hostile slits as his focus shifted from her face to the shirt she was wearing.

Krista couldn't stop the involuntary stiffening of her body when Alexi's hands curled into fists. A small measure of satisfaction returned to Alexi's face when he saw her reaction.

"You have good reason to be frightened, Krista," he said, then turned his attention to his driver. "You have made good on your promise, Mr. Bicos, and returned my property to me. You don't know how much that means to me. Ruben, please give Mr. Bicos his reward."

The man smiled in anticipation and started to turn toward Ruben. He saw his reward in the split second that Krista did. Her scream filled the air as his body slumped to the ground.

Rueben unscrewed the silencer and holstered his gun. Alexi said, "I'll leave you and Marco to see that Mr. Bicos and his motor home are removed from the property."

Ruben nodded and Alexi turned his attention to Krista.

She'd lost the battle with her nausea and stood hunched over, fighting off the horror and the fear.

"It's unfortunate that you had to witness that, Krista. But you needed to understand what your actions wrought. If Mr. Bicos and his associates had found you alone and brought you to me, then I would simply have paid what was owed and moved on. But they found you whoring yourself with two men, Krista. That's not something that I want known about my wife."

Every cell in Krista's body shouted in denial at his claim that she'd be his wife, at the claim that she was responsible for the murder she'd just witnessed, but she kept her head bowed so that he wouldn't see her thoughts. While she was alive, there was hope.

Alexi stepped forward and took Krista's arm in an iron grip before turning back toward the cabin. Instinct screamed for her to fight free of Alexi and make a dash for the woods, but Krista forced herself to still her panic and appear calm. Barefoot and unarmed, she had everything to lose and nothing to gain by attempting escape at the moment.

Behind her the Mercedes and the motor home engines started. She wondered if Alexi's two bodyguards would return to the cabin, or if they had other accommodations. She suspected the latter, glad in this instance of Alexi's possessive jealousy, his need to hoard her like a prize. It had worked to her advantage on the yacht, giving her the chance to steal away unseen and unnoticed because the crew feared having anything to do with her.

As soon as they stepped inside the cabin, Alexi closed the door. Krista had no warning, other than the sting of fabric being wrenched away from her body as Alexi grabbed the shirt and tore it off of her. Instinctually she wanted to try and cover herself, but instead, she forced her arms to stay at her side as she turned to face him.

He was breathing hard, Adan's shirt still gripped in his fist. Krista didn't know whether to be relieved or frightened by the flush that spread across his cheeks as his eyes lowered to view her naked body.

Chapter Thirteen

ഌ

It made Krista's skin crawl to think of him touching her, and yet his desire for her might be the only thing that would keep her alive until she could escape. Regret poured through her. She'd been wrong not to tell Adan and Lyan everything she knew about Alexi. If she had, then maybe they'd be able to track her down here...

Adan and Lyan's voices echoed in her mind, their pledge soul-deep. *You belong to us now. You are ours to pleasure and protect.*

A small hope formed in Krista's heart, so tiny that she didn't dare allow herself to believe fully, but nevertheless, it was enough to feed her inner strength. She stared at Alexi, offering no fear, no emotion.

The flush left his face. Slowly his fist unclenched and Adan's shirt fell to the floor. "When I was eleven, my mother deserted us. She ran away with one of the bodyguards assigned to me. They were found, of course. And dealt with. My father saw to it personally."

Alexi's gaze dropped to Adan's shirt. "Unfortunately, prudence dictated that your lovers meet a swifter and not as satisfying end than I would have preferred. But be assured, Krista, they are both dead."

His attention shifted back to her face. "You have betrayed me three times now. First by going to the police. Then by running away. And now this—spreading your legs for two strangers and letting them mark you." His hand whipped out and struck her across the face with such force that she sank to her knees, too dizzy to stand.

"I wanted you to be my wife, the mother of my children, and you repay me by distrust and deception."

Krista forced herself to look at Alexi. She wouldn't kneel humbly and wait for him to put a bullet in her head.

Alexi's face was flushed, his breath shuddering in and out of his chest. A hard-on pressed against the front of his slacks.

Krista forced her fear down. Even if he raped her, there might be an unguarded moment when she could escape. She made herself get back to her feet and forced herself to speak calmly, as though the cold-blooded murders weren't the reason she'd fled. "You would have wanted me to give up everything else—my job, my friends, my freedom...my chance to live a normal life."

"You don't need anything but me." His arm shot out, his hand moving so fast that Krista stumbled backward in an effort to avoid being hit again. But the expected blow didn't fall. Instead he grabbed her by the neck, his grip strong enough to hurt, but not so strong as to damage muscle and bone. He pulled Krista close to him. Then as abruptly as he'd grabbed her, Alexi let her go. "You stink like a whore, Krista. I can smell them on you. It nauseates me." He pointed toward an open door. Through it Krista could see a bed. She couldn't stop her body from stiffening.

Alexi laughed harshly. "That'll come, if you're lucky and I can overlook your betrayal. For now, you'll take a shower. Then I'll decide whether to keep you naked or let you wear one of the nightgowns I bought you in Paris." He nodded toward the bedroom. Krista moved toward it, already wondering if there was a window that she could escape through.

There was, but it didn't matter. Alexi entered with her and stayed as she stepped into the glassed-in bathing compartment.

"Clean every inch of yourself, Krista," he ordered and she shivered at the slight huskiness in his voice. She knew then that he planned to watch, that she had a decision to make if he wanted to fuck her after she was clean.

Could she stand it? Could she bear to have him touch her? Even if it meant that it'd keep her alive?

Would Lyan and Adan understand if she did? Forgive her? Still want her as their bond-mate?

As the water pounded against her body, Krista tried to ignore Alexi. Tried to ignore the way he'd moved closer to the glass door, how one of his hands slid into his pocket.

Only the voice of reason whispering in Krista's head kept her from laughing and telling him that nothing he had could compare to Adan and Lyan, nothing he could do would bring her the pleasure they'd brought her.

She turned away slightly, preferring to only partially shield herself rather than to turn her back on Alexi completely. Surreptitiously she watched as his eyes followed the movement of her hands as she lathered soap over her body. His face was flushed, the hand in his pocket now obviously manipulating his genitals.

Krista knew that it wouldn't be long now before he'd be ready. She shivered under the hot water, repulsed that once she'd found it pleasing to turn him on.

She didn't think she could stand to have him touch her, especially if he'd done as he said and had Adan and Lyan killed.

The voice of survival screamed in her head. *Act now! Act now while it's just the two of you and he's distracted!*

With every ounce of strength she had, Krista shoved the door to the bathing stall open, slamming it into Alexi. He grunted and stumbled backward but didn't fall down as she'd hoped. One of his hands grabbed her arm but slid off her wet skin.

Krista's heart was pounding in her ears, her only focus on getting through the bathroom door and out of the house. "You'll be sorry for this," Alexi growled, lunging for her.

Out of the corner of her eye she saw something dark in his hand. A weapon.

She tried to dodge but Alexi surged forward and pressed the dark metal to her skin. There was a second of shocked understanding as the stun gun connected and Krista lost the ability to control her limbs. She pitched forward, slamming into the door. Then there was only oblivion.

Chapter Fourteen

SO

Krista came to on a couch in the den, her forehead pounding. It took a moment for her thoughts to line up. Gently she ran her fingers over the knot on her temple, now doubled in size with the second insult in one day. It throbbed and touching it made her stomach and throat tighten as nausea rolled through her.

She was wearing a nightgown now, a soft pink garment that Alexi had given her when she was on the yacht, but it was better than being naked. Her heart raced with renewed hope, with possibility. She was alive and where there was life, there was the chance of escape.

Alexi's presence hovered behind her somewhere, a silent menace. A personal demon waiting to begin tormenting her again.

Cautiously Krista sat up. There was a moment of vertigo then her mind cleared except for the ever-present pounding in her temple.

Her wrists felt raw and sore. The skin was reddened, as though Alexi had tried to remove the bracelets Adan and Lyan had placed on her. Krista rubbed her fingers over the bracelets and Alexi chose that moment to make his presence known.

"Tokens from your dead lovers, Krista? Unfortunately I wasn't able to remove them. They offend me. Rest assured, if I decide to keep you with me, they will be removed and destroyed." His eyes flickered to the bruised, swollen place on Krista's forehead.

Krista braced herself, expecting there to be repercussions from her attempted escape. Instead, Alexi walked over to the bar and poured himself a drink, drawing the tension out. She recognized his game for what it was—*cat and mouse.* She wouldn't give him the satisfaction of playing. That she was alive, relatively unhurt, gave her reason to believe that Alexi wasn't done with her yet, wasn't willing to give up his belief that he could keep her like a possession.

Ice cubes clinked against the side of his glass as he swirled his drink. "You're fortunate that seeing your skin marred with more bruises would repulse me, Krista." His lips twisted in a parody of a smile. "It's a trait I don't share with my father. He demanded complete obedience from my mother and never allowed a transgression to go unpunished. I see now that I've been too lenient with you, too generous. I didn't want you to fear me." He paused for effect then added, "My mistake."

Dread began to fill Krista, but she didn't give him the satisfaction of seeing any reaction.

He smiled, as though he knew what she was doing, and said, "I'm sure you're wondering what I'm going to do to you for ruining my pleasure earlier with your little escape attempt. I could wait and tell you after the fact, but your punishment will be much more effective if you know ahead of time." Alexi laughed. "I don't know why I didn't think of it earlier. It'll be like killing two birds with one stone, or more accurately, by killing one bird, I'll remove several stones from my life—and yours, Krista."

He took a slow sip of his drink before continuing. "You know I don't want to share your affections with anyone. I've made that clear on several occasions."

Horror shimmered along Krista's skin. Her heart thundered in her chest.

Alexi moved away from the bar and walked over to stand in front of her. "I've already taken care of your last two lovers, Krista. Your lack of grief over them makes me think that you were using them. Trading sex for protection. In a way, that makes me feel better—it makes you seem less...sullied. That teacher you dated is another matter, however. It's always bothered me that he survived the hit-and-run accident."

He smiled and saluted her with his glass. "Your punishment, Krista. Ruben is already on his way to San Francisco to deal with your teacher friend."

She made a small sound of pain. She wanted to beg Alexi not to have Matt hurt, yet at the same time she was terrified that doing so would only make it worse for Matt. Alexi had never believed her when she'd told him that Matt was more a friend than anything else.

Alexi put his glass down on a nearby end table. Krista braced herself not to flinch away from his touch, not to show the revulsion, the hatred she felt toward him.

Slowly he stroked smooth fingers across her cheek. "I think we understand each other now. Don't we, Krista?"

She couldn't remain silent, forever wondering if she could have done something to prevent Matt's death. "Please don't have Matt hurt. He's not a part of this. I won't try and run again."

Even as she said it, she knew that it was true. She couldn't keep running. She couldn't live with the ever-present worry that he would track down the people she cared about and destroy them one by one. This was her fight, her mistake for not seeing the monster he was soon enough, and it would end with one of them dead.

Alexi laughed, tracing the outline of her lips then pressing his thumb against the seam in a silent command for her to submit and take a symbolic part of him into her mouth. "Oh, I know you won't run again, Krista. What was the name of that student you were so fond of?" He pressed harder against her lips. "Jessica something. No matter. I'm sure it'll be easy to find her. It's not every day that a girl from her section of town gets singled out for a full scholarship to Harvard."

Krista turned her head away, unable to force herself to yield to his advance, praying that he wouldn't decide to retaliate by hurting the people she cared about for each of her "infractions".

Alexi laughed softly and rubbed his knuckles along her cheek. "You're so beautiful, Krista. From the first moment I saw you, I wanted you and no one else. I hate to have to control and punish you. You should have stayed in the dining room as I instructed that night. Then none of this would have had to happen. We'd be married now and you'd be happily expecting our first child. I never wanted you involved in my business."

"You killed a policeman," Krista said, trying not to let the horror show in her voice.

"I didn't know he was an undercover agent at the time. Over the years I've found it's much easier to pay for evidence and witnesses to disappear, and for policemen to look the other way." Alexi gripped her chin and forced Krista to face him. "We'll spend some time here at the cabin, then we'll go to Nevada and get married before returning to California. My lawyers should have everything settled by them. I'm afraid the DA you've been in contact with is destined for disappointment." He laughed at Krista's small gasp, and said, "For a price, any information can be had, though you were clever enough to be long gone until your last call. Someone on my payroll traced you to Las Vegas. From there it was easy to guess where else you might go." Alexi smiled slightly. "I hope you've learned your lesson, Krista. There's nowhere you can go that I can't eventually find you. There's no one you can trust that can't be bought or killed." He smiled slightly. "I think we understand each other now. From now on, all you have to worry about is pleasing me."

Krista's stomach churned and her head throbbed, she ran the fingertips of one hand over the knot on her forehead. Alexi's eyes narrowed, but she couldn't be sure whether it was at the sight of Lyan's bracelet or because her injury reminded him of the escape attempt.

An idea flashed in Krista's mind. She licked her lips and Alexi's gaze dropped to follow the movement.

Steeling herself to play a role, she leaned forward, as though she was going to nuzzle the front of his pants in supplication. But before her face could make contact, she swayed slightly and closed her eyes.

"I feel a little dizzy." She touched the knot on her forehead again. "A hot compress would help. And something to eat. I haven't eaten since yesterday."

Alexi studied her silently for several long seconds before saying, "Very well, Krista. We can take care of your needs first. Then we'll take care of mine. I've eased myself with other women since you betrayed me, but they were poor substitutes for you."

He stood back and allowed Krista to rise. She didn't need to fake the slight stumble as she took a step away from the sofa. Out of the corner of her eye she saw Alexi's hand twitch and move slightly toward the pocket of his sports jacket. If she was right, then that's where the stun gun was.

Her mind whirled, trying to calculate probabilities. Could she get to it and use it on Alexi? Even if she could, would the stun be enough to immobilize him? How long would she have to… Her mind shied away from finishing the thought but Krista resolutely forced herself back to visualizing his murder. She knew that people died from stun guns. Once he was immobilized, she'd figure out what needed to be done.

Her heart pounded in her throat. There would only be one chance to kill Alexi. If she failed, then he would either dispose of her on the spot, or he'd ensure that she never had another chance to murder him.

And if he kept her alive, she didn't doubt that he'd torture her by killing anyone he thought she might care about. She shivered in fear and desperation. She wouldn't be able to avoid his sexual demands very much longer, but compared to being the cause of his murdering innocent people, her own suffering would pale in comparison.

They stepped into the kitchen. Alexi halted near the table, leaning casually against it as his hand slipped into his jacket pocket. Krista moved to the refrigerator, opening it so that she could use the door to shield her survey of the room. A cutting board was on the counter near the sink. Next to it was a collection of cooking knives sheathed in a wooden block.

She knew immediately that Alexi was testing her. Seeing if she was desperate enough—or foolish enough—to go for one of the knives. She selected a container of egg salad from the refrigerator, dug around in the cabinet for bread, then selected a dull table knife from a drawer within arm's reach of the cooking knives.

Krista took her supplies to the table and made a sandwich, only to find after the first bite that she really was starving. She made a second sandwich in order to dull the hunger and delay the inevitable moment when she'd have to either give in to Alexi's demands or strike against him.

She knew that she didn't stand a chance if he decided to rape her, and she suspected that even if she could bring herself to willingly have sex with him, he wouldn't simply doze off afterward and leave her to wander freely around the house.

He'd have other weapons here, guns probably, and they would be no use to him locked up so that he couldn't get to them quickly. He wouldn't take the chance that she would find one. The fact that he'd kept his hand in his pocket, on the stun gun, while she rummaged around near the block full of cooking knives proved to Krista that even though he thought he could hold her by fear, he didn't trust her not to try and escape again.

Once he'd gotten his sexual gratification, Alexi would lock her up, or tie her up, and she'd be helpless to do anything…and Matt would die. Bile burned Krista's throat at the thought.

She rose from her chair and returned to the counter, replacing the bread and washing the knife and plate she'd used, then putting them up. She couldn't see Alexi, but she could sense his heightened alertness.

Her heart thundered in her chest at what she was preparing to do, at the risk and possible consequences. But she had no choice. She had to escape. She had to kill Alexi before he could order more deaths. She had to somehow prevent her friend's death.

She rubbed her temple before taking a clean dishtowel out of the drawer and soaking it with hot water. Once the compress was in place on her forehead, she said, "Can you massage the back of my head and my neck? I think that'd make the pain go away more quickly."

There was a slight hesitation, as though she'd caught Alexi by surprise with her request. "Come over here," he said.

"It'd be better if we could do it near the sink, so I can keep the compress hotter."

Krista held her breath as she waited to see what he would do. Her heart began pounding in her ears when she heard his footsteps moving across the ceramic kitchen floor. *Could she do this? Could she physically attack him? Could she actually kill him?* She shuddered, her mind coming to the same conclusion it had earlier. She didn't have any choice.

Alexi stopped behind her. She could feel his body heat along her back. Krista lowered her head, offering him her neck as she reached forward, turning on the hot water and refreshing the compress.

Once again Alexi hesitated. This time he was close enough that she could feel the tension in his body. When she did nothing other than squeeze out the dishcloth and press it against her forehead, he slowly relaxed and lifted one hand to her neck.

Krista sighed and leaned back slightly so that her buttocks rested against his groin. She forced herself to press into him as though she welcomed the feel of his body against hers, his erection against her nightgown-covered flesh.

There was the soft sound of skin against fabric as he removed his other hand from his pocket and brought it to her shoulder, kneading and rubbing. Once again she refreshed the compress. Alexi tensed but didn't reach for the stun gun.

Krista refreshed the compress several times. With each repeated action, Alexi tensed less and less, but she knew that even with his cock pressing against her buttocks, he would not drop his guard completely again.

The hand massaging the back of her skull traveled down to brush against her nipple and then her hip. Krista knew that time was rapidly running out. She reached again for the faucet, using both hands to ring out the dishcloth several times, as though it wasn't getting hot enough. Alexi's breathing was more noticeable as he rubbed himself against her.

Krista prayed for courage and luck as she let the dishcloth become saturated with scalding hot water. When she could delay no longer, she swung around, slapping the water-soaked towel into Alexi's face with all her might before grabbing a knife and stabbing him.

He fell backward, yelling in outrage. She attacked, following him down to the floor, her fear giving her strength.

But it was not enough.

He managed to fling her backward and get the stun gun out of his pocket as she scrambled to her feet. There was so much blood that for a second Krista thought she'd hit one of his arteries. But then he stood and his eyes held a murderous rage.

He was between her and the doorway. Water and blood pouring off him. Krista's heart was pounding so hard that it felt like it was going to explode in her chest.

Alexi moved forward, stumbling slightly. Krista grabbed the heavy cutting board and threw it at him. He blocked it with his arm, grunting as it struck him.

She got a second knife from the holder, this one larger than the first had been. Alexi moved a step closer. She held both knifes in front of her, ready to use both to defend herself. He held the stun gun away from his body as he prepared to close in on her.

Chapter Fifteen

ഌ

Krista's breath was shuddering in and out of her chest. Her mind was trying to read his body language and calculate his moves. She couldn't let him touch her with the stun gun.

A crash came from the other room. Alexi halted, a surprised look flickering across his face. He yelled out, "Ruben? Marco?"

Krista almost dropped her knives when Lyan appeared in the doorway to the kitchen. Alexi whirled to face the intruder and Krista moved quickly, plunging the knife into his back even as her soul recoiled in horror at what she was doing.

He screamed in fury and started to turn back toward Krista. She pulled the knife out, ready to repeat the attack, desperate to finish it before Adan or Lyan got hurt.

The stun gun sparked against Adan's wristband and he laughed as he continued forward, ready to kill this man who had threatened the life of their bond-mate. Lyan's voice halted him. *I claim this kill by right of the Fallon gene marker that makes Krista mine by Council decree.*

Despite the seriousness of the situation, amusement rushed through Adan at the outrageousness of Lyan claiming a right based on the very Council he'd so often ignored and railed against. He laughed and moved quickly, taking Krista into his arms before she could risk being injured by attacking Alexi again, then said, *Yours by right, but do it now.*

Lyan swung his arm, knocking the stun gun out of Alexi's hand as though it was a plastic toy. He followed by driving his fist into Alexi's gut. As Alexi hunched forward in reaction, Lyan grabbed him by the head and twisted. There was the sickening sound of bones breaking and soft tissue being torn.

When Lyan released his hold, Alexi's body dropped to the kitchen floor, face slack, eyes staring, body voiding itself.

Krista whimpered and buried her face in Adan's chest. The knives in her hands clattered to the floor and she began shaking uncontrollably.

Lyan pressed his body against her back. His arms joined Adan's, holding her, cocooning her in the warmth of their love and their protection.

"I am sorry you had to witness that, beloved," Lyan whispered against her hair.

"I was so afraid." Krista's voice was a mere thread of sound.

"You are safe now," Adan said, also nuzzling her hair.

Krista shivered again and both Lyan and Adan began stroking her body, offering reassurance even as they checked her for injuries.

"He said he'd had you killed. I tried not to believe it, but I was so scared that it was true."

Adan laughed. "The ones he sent were no match for us. We took care of them quickly and came for you."

"How did you know where I was?"

Lyan pressed his lips against her neck in a soft kiss. "You belong to us. You are ours to pleasure and protect. Our bond-mate. There is nowhere you can go that we can not find you. It is time to complete the binding and take you home with us. Never again will you know this kind of fear." He moved away and said, "Adan will take you to the place we have chosen for the binding. I will deal with this mess."

Krista pulled away from Adan's arms. "I can't leave yet. I need to go to San Francisco. Alexi sent someone to kill Matt, the teacher I told you about." Her heart raced as she remembered that Alexi had a second bodyguard. "There was someone else guarding Alexi."

Lyan laughed. "We have already disposed of that threat."

Adan leaned forward and rubbed his nose along Krista's. "Do you trust us to protect your friend from harm?"

Krista could only nod. She did trust them. With her life. With Matt's life.

Adan rewarded her with a smile so full of joy that her chest tightened and burned with emotion. "I love you," she whispered. "I love you both so much that I don't think I'd want to go on without you."

"It is the same for us. In all the universe, you are the only one for us." Adan pressed her against his body, stroking her back and holding her as though she was his world. When he released her he said, "Come, let us leave Lyan to do what needs to be done here. He will join us shortly."

When Krista turned, Lyan pulled her forward so that their bodies touched. He pressed his forehead to hers and stroked her cheek gently. "Do you know who this man is that has been sent to hurt your friend?"

A picture of Ruben came immediately to Krista's mind. "Yes. Alexi's driver. His name is Ruben. I don't know his last name, but he's worked for Alexi for a long time."

Lyan brushed Krista's lips with his own. "Do not worry for your friend. Adan and I both have brothers and cousins who can go to San Francisco. I will send word to them and they will go immediately to protect your friend and eliminate this threat."

Krista shivered. Part of her was appalled at how easy it was to accept this violence in her life. But she couldn't bring herself to plead for leniency on Ruben's behalf.

Adan moved so that his body molded itself to her back while Lyan still pressed against her front. Warmth and heat flooded her, and once again she felt surrounded by them, protected by them, loved by them.

A different kind of shiver ran through her. Adan pushed closer, letting her feel his answering need. Lyan's laugh was husky as he stroked her cheek and lowered his mouth to hover above hers. "Go now with Adan. The next time we join it will bind us together forever."

Krista leaned forward and pressed a kiss against Lyan's lips before saying, "Please be careful." He chuckled and Krista allowed Adan to lead her away from the cabin.

She was momentarily disoriented when she saw her car parked next to one of Alexi's sports cars. Adan opened the passenger door and she got in, suddenly overwhelmed by so many emotions that she began shaking again.

"All will be well," Adan said as he bent down and hugged her to him. "Soon we will be home."

In his warm embrace, the turbulent emotions gradually faded and more practical concerns surfaced. Krista pulled away slightly and said, "I'm still in a nightgown."

Adan lifted his eyebrows and grinned. "A very transparent nightgown. It suits you, though it is quite distracting."

Krista laughed and more of the horror of the day slipped away. "I think I'd better change."

"I will get you something to wear."

Adan gently closed the passenger door before retrieving a pair of jeans and a shirt from one of her suitcases in the trunk of the car and handing it to her as he took the driver's seat. She cocked an eyebrow and asked, "No underwear?" He chuckled and started the engine.

Krista laughed then sobered as she began changing and noticed Alexi's blood spattered on her arms and on the front of the nightgown. Thankfully there was a half-empty water bottle in the holder on her dash. She used it to clean Alexi's blood from her skin. The moment she was finished dressing, Adan reached over and took her hand in his. Krista clung to it, drawing strength and warmth from him.

She'd expected Adan to head for one of the highways that would lead to Sacramento or back to Reno. Instead, he stuck to winding, scarcely used roads. After they'd traveled for a while, Krista finally asked, "Where are we going?"

He smiled. "You will see soon enough."

Krista's heart lightened for no reason at all other than she loved his smile, his presence. She tightened her grip on his hand, then leaned over to trail the fingers of her free hand along the inside of his thigh. "I have ways of making you talk," she teased. "Where are we going?"

Beneath her fingers she could feel his body tense. With her own eyes she could see the bulge in his pants become more pronounced.

Adan shuddered when her fingers moved the final distance and covered his erection. He wanted to pull to the side of the road and make love to her. He wanted to hear her screams of pleasure, to pound into her until neither of them could move any longer.

He wanted to rid himself completely of the terror that had gripped him when Krista had disappeared. There had been no doubt in his mind that they would find her and get her back, but he had feared what might happen to her before they could reach her.

Her touch was driving him crazy. But he would not take her again until the binding ceremony. On that, he and Lyan had agreed before they had stormed into Alexi's cabin.

Adan exhaled harshly. His cock was so hard it throbbed. His hand had a death grip on the steering wheel. He ached to open his pants and free his erection, to bury his hands in Krista's hair as she took him first into her mouth and then into her hot, tight sheath.

She laughed softly, seductively and Adan's hips pumped involuntarily. "Maybe you should pull over to the side of the road," Krista told him.

"Krista," he groaned. "We must wait for the binding ceremony."

She tightened her grip on him, massaging up and down his length. Her touch searing him through his clothing.

"Why wait?" she whispered.

His cock jerked in her grip. "Lyan and I agreed that neither of us would take you again until we could do so together."

What had started as play had quickly spun out of Krista's control. Her nipples were tight and needy, her cunt was swollen and wet. Krista wanted to wrap herself around Adan, to feel him deep inside of her, affirming that she was safe and loved.

"But I didn't agree not to take you," she said as she pulled his zipper down and freed his cock.

"Krista," he groaned again, desperate for her mouth, unable to stop himself from moving closer to her lips as her hot breath moved across the engorged head of his penis.

In response she slid her fingers along his length until they cupped his scrotum. Her wet, silky tongue gently probed the tiny hole that was already leaking in his excitement.

Adan jerked against her. She was killing him with her touch. Never had he experienced this kind of agony. This kind of pleasure.

He groaned again, tormented by need, but not wanting to violate the oath he'd taken with Lyan. They were both so close to merging completely with Krista. To do so when apart might mean there could be no shared bond-mate. "Krista, we must wait. To do otherwise might hurt Lyan."

Krista heard the desperation and sincerity in his voice. She pulled away, her body aching and unfulfilled, but the thought of hurting Lyan was intolerable to her. "How much further is this place you're taking me to?"

"It is not far." With a grimace, he managed to pull his pants closed over his massive erection. "Lyan will catch up to us soon. That I can promise you. The hunger we feel burns in him as well."

Krista squeezed her legs together and nodded. "Then let's hurry and get there."

Adan once again took her hand in his. His thumb brushed across her knuckles as he said, "You are more than I ever hoped for in a bond-mate, more than I ever thought to deserve."

Love rushed through Krista, smoothing the sexual heat into something much gentler though no less consuming. "I'm the lucky one to have you and Lyan," she said as she snuggled against Adan until they reached their destination.

By some miracle, Lyan was already there. He lounged casually in front of an old, adobe-style building. Krista's heart quickened when she saw him and the last of the fear she'd been holding inside slipped away.

Adan parked the car and watched as Krista rushed to embrace Lyan. *All went well?* he asked.

Lyan lifted an arrogant eyebrow before burying his face in Krista's hair. *Of course. Now let us begin so that we can take our bond-mate and leave this primitive planet! I have already been inside and done what is necessary.*

Renewed hunger rushed through Adan. His heartbeat accelerated. The moment he had long dreamed of was upon them.

Lyan pulled away from Krista as Adan joined them. The purple crystal in his wristbands began to hum and pulse in time with the throbbing in his cock. He could see the swirl of gold in the crystals Adan wore and knew that they vibrated in tune to Adan's emotion and in proximity to the crystals inside the portal chamber. Soon the purple and gold crystals would be in sync and the binding would take place. Soon Krista would be in their home, theirs for all time.

Krista was surprised when they stepped inside the adobe building. She'd expected to walk into the living room of a small cottage. Instead she was in an intimate, terraced garden. Above her head, the ceiling was see-through to allow the sun to shine on an exquisite collection of flowering plants. Beneath her feet were colorful stones arranged in exotic patterns. In the center of the room, amid a spectacular pattern of crystals, was a thick mattress on a frame that rested close to the ground.

Adan brushed his fingertips across Krista's cheek, then lowered his hand and began unbuttoning her shirt. Next to her, Lyan removed his clothing and dropped it in a wooden chest by the door. Krista shivered—in part from anticipation, in part from fear. Doubt tried to press in on her as she took in the ceremonial nature of this place, the oddness of it being out here in the middle of nowhere.

Adan removed her shirt and dropped it in the wooden chest where Lyan's clothes had been placed. As if sensing her growing fear, he said, "Do not be afraid, Krista. Trust us."

There was a tremor in her voice as she answered, "I do."

Lyan knelt in front of her. He pressed a hot, wet kiss against the bare flesh of Krista's stomach as his hands went to her jeans, opening them and pulling them down her legs. He rubbed his nose down the sensitive skin of her belly, stopping when it nestled in the soft down between her legs.

With a groan, Lyan held her steady as he lifted one of her feet and then the other so that he could remove her jeans. Next to them, Adan had already removed his shirt and pants. He swooped her jeans up and deposited them with the rest of the clothing. "It is time," he growled and the fierce need in his voice shot through Krista like a bolt of lightning. Involuntarily her legs clinched together as her labia became more engorged.

Lyan pressed his face closer and the heat of his breath against her wet, aching sex made her grind into him and clutch at his shoulders. His hands came around to grip her buttocks, holding her while his mouth sought and found her stiff, fully erect clitoris.

Krista whimpered with need. She quivered, wanting him to suck her.

Underneath her fingers, the muscles in Lyan's shoulders bunched and tightened. Then with a groan, he pulled himself away from her and stood.

Krista cried out at the loss of his wet mouth. Her gaze traveled automatically to his groin. Lyan's erection was fierce, firm, already glistening with drops of his need.

Without speaking a word, Lyan and Adan each took one of her hands and led her to the bed in the center of the garden. Standing next to it, Adan turned her to face him, pressing his lower body against hers while Lyan moved to wrap himself around her from behind.

"Once the binding ceremony is complete then we must take you home with us," Adan said, his eyes meeting and holding hers, his expression somber though his face was taut with need. "There is no going back once this is done."

Lyan's grip tightened around her waist. *It is already too late to go back*, he growled in Adan's mind.

The panic that had driven Krista from her cabin and allowed Alexi's men to capture her returned full force. Lyan and Adan wanted to take her to their home, and yet she had no idea where their home was. If she went home with them, would she disappear, never to be seen again?

As if sensing her panic, both Lyan and Adan bent closer, nuzzling kisses against her skin. "All will be well, beloved," Adan whispered.

"Do not think to leave us," Lyan warned, his teeth closing on the bite mark he'd given her.

Krista's heart beat so fast, she knew they could probably hear it. She licked her lips and asked, "Where's your home?"

Adan kissed his way up her neck until his lips hovered over hers. "Far from here. That is all that I can tell you."

"And once I'm there, I can't leave. Right?"

Adan frowned. "I have never heard of a bond-mate wishing to leave."

"What if I want to come back and visit my friends, will I be able to?"

"I do not know." Adan stroked her cheek. "You are ours to pleasure and protect. If it is within our power, know that Lyan and I will do anything to make you happy."

Krista leaned into his hand as the last of her panic fled. She loved them. She trusted them. She wanted nothing more than to be theirs forever.

"Let's do the binding ceremony then so that we can go home," she said, pressing her buttocks against Lyan's erection while at the same time moving her hand down so that she could brush her thumb across the head of Adan's cock.

Both men groaned but instead of pushing her down to the bed, they surprised Krista by stepping away from her. Adan's voice was soft as he said, "See us as we really are, Krista."

The gold crystal in his wristbands pulsed and swirled, and then the air shimmered behind Adan's back as though thousands of molecules were suddenly gathering in one place. They sparkled in the air like gauzy fabric until finally becoming solid.

Krista's heart pounded in her chest at the sight of Adan standing there with his glorious golden-veined wings. She couldn't stop herself from moving into him and brushing her hand against their feathery perfection.

His eyelids dropped and he shivered in sensual pleasure as she pressed her hands against the muscled underside and stroked along the edges. "I dreamed of this," Krista whispered. "I dreamed that we made love and you looked like this. Like an angel."

Adan's laugh was slightly husky. "Why am I not surprised that once again Lyan has disregarded Council law."

Lyan growled. "I did not knowingly show Krista our true form. If she saw it, it is because of the Fallon gene she carries."

Krista's eyebrows drew together in puzzlement. "What are you talking about?"

"Later," Adan said and looked behind her at Lyan.

Krista turned and saw Lyan as she'd seen him in her dreams, with wings like those of a bat.

He was the opposite of Adan's golden beauty. The demon to Adan's angel. And yet Lyan was every bit as desirable to her.

The uncertainty on his face made Krista's heart ache and she went to him immediately. He stiffened, as though he feared she'd be repulsed.

Krista laughed softly and ran her hands over the soft black suede of his wings until his eyelids dropped in pleasure. Something tickled at the edge of Krista's mind and she said, "There's more, isn't there?"

Lyan slowly lifted his lip and his fangs descended. Krista touched the spot on her neck where Lyan had repeatedly bitten her. "That's how you found me in Reno, and at Alexi's cabin. You took my blood and now you can track me anywhere."

Lyan's face twisted in disgust. "I am Vesti, not the vampire of your human legends."

Krista laughed and pulled his head down so that she could run her tongue along the length of one of his fangs. Lyan's nostrils flared and his cock jerked against her stomach. "But you did something," she said, teasing him by running her tongue along the second fang.

He shivered under her attention. "The mating fangs of the Vesti inject a serum so that we can track our mates. It is not necessary to bite more than once, but it brings pleasure to both of us, so I continue to do it."

Krista released him and moved so that she could look at both of them. "This doesn't change anything. I love you both. I want to be with you wherever you are."

"Then let us complete the binding ceremony and go home," Adan said as each of them took one of her hands and settled her on the bed.

Krista slid across the plush bedding until she was in the center. Adan and Lyan followed, taking only a second to push her onto her back as they situated themselves on either side of her.

Krista's heart beat in anticipation. She was wet for them, swollen and ready...needy. A whimper escaped as first Adan, then Lyan kissed her, their lips first soothing, then possessive.

In a synchronized movement, they left her lips and traveled downward, kissing and biting her neck as they went. Her nipples tightened to aching points in anticipation of their mouths. She couldn't stop herself from arching upward as they each latched on to a pink areola.

Her legs moved restlessly, widening to invite their attention. Against her breast, Adan laughed softly, seductively, before answering her siren's call with his fingers.

A sob escaped from Krista and she pressed her throbbing clit harder against Adan's palm. He rewarded her by grinding his hand against her and stroking his fingers in and out of her slit. Lyan's fingers moved to trace along the dark cleft between her buttocks. Reflexively Krista arched away from the touch. He growled against her nipple, biting down in warning and she shivered, remembering the wildness of when he'd taken her there, remembering whispered words of what they had planned for her during the binding ceremony.

Krista's hands dug into their silky hair and along the top edges of their wings, alternating between trying to pull one of them back to her mouth and trying to push one of them down to her aching cunt. "Please," she whimpered, and Adan returned to her lips while Lyan kissed and licked his way down to her hungry, wet slit. As soon as Lyan's tongue sank into her opening, Adan's slid into her mouth. In symphony they drove into her wet depths, then retreated to bite and suckle on swollen lips. When she would have driven herself harder against Lyan's mouth, they held her down as they teased and tormented her, repeatedly taking Krista closer and closer to orgasm without letting her go over.

Adan's rigid cock was pressed against her thigh. She rubbed against it, wanted to feel it inside her, wanting to feel both of them inside her, taking her as Lyan had vowed they would, binding them together as he'd promised.

Her body was covered in sweat and she burned for their possession. When Adan pulled away from her mouth, she begged, shivering, shuddering, desperate for them to plunge their cocks into her body and make her theirs. "I need you both. I need you both inside me."

Lyan groaned and took one last greedy lick before leaving her cunt and rising so that his face was above hers. He was flushed, his eyes dilated with lust and his lips swollen and wet from pleasuring her. "Now," he said, baring his teeth.

"Now," Adan echoed, lying on his back, his wings fluffed across the bed like a huge pillow.

He shifted Krista so that she was on top of him, legs spread and resting against the downy softness of his wings as his hungry erection pressed against her opening.

Krista whimpered, overwhelmed by the erotic combination of soft wing and hard man. She reached down, grasping his cock in her hands and guiding it to her flooded slit. With a groan he shoved himself into her, but when Krista would have levered herself up so that she could pleasure them both on his engorged flesh, Adan held her against him, his hands moving to spread her buttocks, opening her for Lyan.

Her body tensed in anticipation, in nervousness. There was only a second's pause before Lyan's oil-coated fingers traveled along the crease of her ass, first circling the puckered hole, then slipping inside, bringing a wake of fire with them.

Some of the lubricant slid to her already penis-filled cunt. Beneath her, Adan thrust in and out of her, coating himself with the potent ritzca oil and then setting Krista's pussy on fire with it.

Adan and Krista both moaned in pleasure as every sensation was intensified. Adan arched upward and this time it was he who growled, "Now!"

Lyan's fingers slipped out of Krista and were immediately replaced by the tip of his cock. He groaned as he slowly worked himself into her nearly virgin entrance, pleasure rippling through his wings as they opened and dropped to form a private lover's tent over the bonding mates.

Krista whimpered, overwhelmed by the intensity of the experience, by the eroticism of their wings, and by the sheer joy of having both of her lovers inside of her at once.

Adan's hands clasped Krista's, positioning them on the bed so that his wristbands touched hers. When Lyan's hands meshed with theirs and his wristbands rested against theirs, both men began to move, slowly at first, then with greater force as they whispered words of need and love and promise.

Krista gave herself over to them completely, returning their words of need and love and promise. And when climax took the three of them, Krista felt connected to them in a way that she'd never felt before, as though they were so closely bound that they could read each other's minds, experience each other's emotions.

Her body still shuddered with pleasure moments later when they shifted onto their sides, their cocks still penetrating her as she lay protected in the warm cocoon of arms and wings.

Krista slid her hand down Adan's arm and noticed that the band on her wrist now contained woven purple and gold stone. She'd thought they were crystals, but now she somehow knew that they were something else—something alien.

The thought made her laugh. Not alien, but something else, that was for sure. Lyan and Adan were the stuff of legends.

She nuzzled Adan's chest and wondered about where their home was. They'd both driven her car, both moved around as though they were familiar with everyday life. They'd both killed to defend her.

Krista's mind shied away from thoughts of Alexi. She rested her forehead on Adan's chest, reassured by the steady beat of his heart. She stroked the underside of his wings and felt his cock stir.

Obviously both Lyan and Adan could appear like normal humans, though she could see why they'd want to live privately. If she had wings...

Krista's heart sped up. Her eyes flew first to the strange crystals in her own wristbands and then to Adan's face.

He stroked her cheek. *Lyan and I will be your wings. The binding ceremony has been completed. As you learn our ways, you will learn the nature of the Ylan crystals and how to use them.*

It took a second for her to realize that his lips hadn't moved. Lyan's hand covered hers where it rested on Adan's wing. *Anyone who sees the purple and gold worn in bands bearing the devices of our two houses will know who protects and cherishes you.*

Over the rush of blood in her head, an outrageous idea began forming in her mind. Krista forced a thought toward Lyan, *Am I really hearing you?*

Both men chuckled, but it was Adan who said, *Is it so hard to believe that life exists beyond this primitive planet you call Earth?*

Out loud, Lyan said, "It is the way of our people to communicate mind-to-mind. Adan and I will help you gain control of your thoughts so that you do not broadcast all that you think." He brushed the tips of his fangs against her flesh, purring with satisfaction when she whimpered and tightened on his still-embedded cock. *Not that I would mind having others know the pleasure you feel at our touch.*

Krista tried to make sense of what they were telling her. The thought of them being alien didn't horrify or scare her. She wasn't just a math teacher, she was a mathematician and also a gambler who understood the odds of certain events happening.

She'd never doubted that life existed on other planets and in other universes. It had always seemed statistically impossible that Earth would house the *only* life. But the odds of this other life looking human...and arriving on Earth...

No, not just arriving. They must have been here all along or at least for thousands of years, which would explain why they'd been depicted in ancient artwork.

Adan stroked her hair. *You are correct. Long ago our ancestors visited here freely...before laws were passed against interfering with cultures not as advanced as our own.*

Krista remembered what Lyan had said earlier and her heart sped up. "The Fallon?"

Adan chuckled and said to Lyan. *It pleases me that we have such an intelligent mate.*

"I heard that," Krista said, the compliment making her feel less overwhelmed by their splendor.

Lyan nuzzled and pressed kisses along her neck. *The Fallon are what the Vesti and Amato once were before pride and arrogance caused separate races to evolve from one great race. They are the common ancestor we all share.*

Adan rubbed his nose along Krista's. *Even you, beloved. Like the Vesti and the Amato of ancient times, some among the Fallon were attracted to your planet. It is because of those long-ago travelers that you carry genes that make you a match for Lyan and me.* His face turned serious. *The hope of both the Vesti and the Amato now lies in those who carry the Fallon genes. Without them, there will be no children for either race and we will slowly die out.*

Krista studied his face and reached out with her mind to touch his emotions, and then Lyan's, wondering if maybe they only wanted her because she could give them children. Their denial was instant, vehement, and Krista let the second of uncertainty fade forever. Only love and a hope for the future filled their hearts and minds.

"So the Fallon are extinct?" Krista asked, trying to fit the pieces of the equation together.

Adan's heart filled with pride and joy at her acceptance of her new world, her desire to understand it better. "Yes. They were a great race of winged shape-shifters able to take many different forms."

She explored one of Adan's feathers with her fingers. "We saw them as angels and demons?"

Pleasure rippled through him at her touch. "To some they were also dragons or faeries or ancient gods."

Krista laughed softly. "Or vampires."

Lyan growled and gently bit her shoulder.

Heat surged through her with the bite and she stroked first Adan's wing, then Lyan's. They shivered under her hand and despite the orgasm she'd just experienced, she wanted them again. She wanted the exquisite intimacy that joining with them brought.

Adan leaned over and pressed his lips to hers. *There will be a lifetime of such joinings. I would stay buried in your cunt and live there forever.*

Lyan ran his mating fangs along her neck. *Do not fear, Krista. When we get you to our home, you will not leave our bed for days.*

The stones around the bed began to pulse in a sequence of light and color. The air in the chamber became charged and Krista's heartbeat accelerated as the strange crystals in her wristbands seemed to pull on the energy around her.

Both men tightened their grip on her, sending reassurance and images of what was about to happen. But even though she knew it was perfectly safe, her heart still raced, giddy with the same fear and exhilaration she felt when she sat in the front seat of a roller coaster and raised her hands. She laughed out loud, unable to stop herself from saying, *Beam me up, Scotty!* as the moment of transport grew closer.

In her mind Lyan's voice growled with possessiveness, *There had better be no Scotty waiting for you.*

Krista grinned, and seemingly between one heartbeat and the next, she moved from one world to the next.

And yet initially, the worlds looked exactly the same.

They were in the center of a room, on a mattress that rested close to the ground, amid a spectacular pattern of crystals. Around them was an intimate, terraced garden, filled with an exquisite collection of flowering plants.

Are you ready to see Winseka? Adan asked as he reluctantly pulled out of Krista's body and stood.

From behind her, Lyan hugged Krista, then also pulled away and stood. *Come, let us get home before our families descend and make it impossible for us to make love to our bond-mate.*

Krista let them help her from the bed. They moved, as though retracing their earlier steps, but instead of finding the clothing they'd been wearing on Earth in the wooden chest, Lyan pulled out a pair of almost sheer purple and gold harem-like pants and knelt in front of Krista. She lifted one foot at a time, shivering in sensual pleasure when his warm hands brushed over her skin along with the silky fabric as he helped her dress.

When she looked up, Adan was dressed in something that looked very much like a gold-colored loincloth made of the same material. Krista flushed at the picture he made, at what the small piece of clothing both concealed and revealed.

Adan laughed and stretched his wings out. *The clothes worn on Earth would only hamper our flight.*

Lyan dressed in a cloth made of purple before taking Krista's hand as though he meant to lead her from the building.

This time the color that flooded Krista's face was embarrassment. "I can't go out like this!"

Lyan's brows drew together. *This is our binding day, it is a tradition that we wear these colors. You can choose another color tomorrow.*

More color rushed to Krista's face. *My breasts aren't covered.*

Lyan's gaze moved immediately to her breasts and Krista's nipples tightened in response. When he moved forward and stroked over one hard areola with his fingers, she couldn't stop a small moan from escaping.

Our women do not cover their breasts, Lyan said as he bent over and took the nipple in his mouth. Krista moaned again and threaded her hand through his hair, holding him to her.

Adan moved to the other breast, taking only a moment to tease the nipple with his tongue before latching onto it and sucking. *From your body will come our children. From your breasts will come the milk to sustain them. Our culture worships both and so our women do not hide their breasts in shame.*

Krista whimpered and pressed into them, their words and their attention making her wet and needy.

Lyan and Adan grasped her pants and pulled until they lay in a silky pool at Krista's feet. Then in perfect sync, their hands moved to her already dripping cunt and they began pleasuring her, stroking her throbbing clit and pressing in and out of her vagina as they continued to suckle at her breasts.

Krista was helpless against their onslaught. Her moans and whimpers filled the chamber, until finally she cried out in release.

Adan left her nipple and kissed upward until his lips covered hers.

Lyan left her nipple and kissed downward until his lips found her still-swollen labia.

As Adan's tongue pierced through the seam of Krista's lips, Lyan's forged into her tight channel, driving her up to another orgasm, before he gently lapped her clean and pulled her pants back into place.

Krista was too weak with pleasure to protest when they took her hands and led her through the door. Somehow she'd been expecting that they would end up outside, as they would have been on Earth, but instead she found herself in a larger room very much like the one they'd just left, with clear ceilings that allowed light to bathe the exotic plants and bounce off the multicolored crystal walls and floor.

A man rose from a bench and Krista's breath caught in her throat. Except for the hard, unforgiving features and the body that seemed to tense, as though bracing for pain, he could have been Adan's twin. Instinctively her mind touched Adan's and found his concern for his brother.

"Zeraac," Adan said, releasing Krista's hand and moving to grip the other man's forearms so that the wristbands they wore touched. When the greeting ended, Adan returned to Krista's side, taking her hand in his once again. "This is our bond-mate, Krista."

Zeraac stepped forward and Krista saw that his eyes were darker than Adan's, a deep well of anguish where Adan's were full of hope and promise. Zeraac pressed his lips to hers, not teasing or coaxing her to open her mouth for him as Lyan's cousin had done.

"Welcome." He stepped back as quickly as he'd moved forward.

"You go to San Francisco?" Adan asked and Krista could sense his desire to divert Zeraac from another more dangerous destination.

"No, Lyan's brother has already attended to the matter." Zeraac's gaze shifted to Krista. "You need not worry for your friends any longer. The one named Ruben has been dealt with."

Krista shivered. Even a world away from Alexi, even knowing that he was dead, she couldn't completely escape the fear that had caused her to run for her life. What if Rueben had told Alexi's father or uncles that she'd been the last person to see Alexi alive? What if they thought she was still running and decided to make examples of her co-workers, her friends, her students in an effort to draw her out? Tears formed and suddenly she felt selfish for coming here, for thinking that it was all over. How could she...

Adan pressed a kiss to her temple, her eyelids, before gently lapping up her tears. *Stop, beloved. All will be well. Did Lyan and I not promise to do all in our power to make you happy? This is an easy thing for us to see to.* He turned to his brother and said, "Our mate fears for those she has left behind. Will you see to their protection?"

"There is no need. It is already being taken care of. When Lyan's message arrived, there were plenty of volunteers anxious to deal with your bond-mate's enemies and see Earth for themselves."

Krista felt Adan's fear for his brother rise and her mind whirled, trying to find something she could ask of him. It came to her in a stab of remembered horror and anguish. Pulling out of Adan and Lyan's grasp, she took Zeraac's hand in hers. "I witnessed the murder of a policeman. His name was Colin Ripa. Would you check to make sure that his wife and child are...that they don't lack for anything?" Her heart ached, knowing that material possessions would never replace a husband, a father, but she couldn't change what had happened.

Zeraac nodded—reluctantly—and Krista felt some of Adan's worry ease. "I will go now." He tilted his head slightly, in acknowledgement of Lyan, then moved into the portal chamber that they'd just left.

Adan brushed a kiss against Krista's lips. *You did well to give him a task, perhaps he will find something worth living for on Earth.*

I will send word to my brothers and ask that they try and involve him in other matters while he is in San Francisco, Lyan said.

They left the building then and Krista's worry and fear faded at the sight of the crystal city surrounding them.

This is Winseka, Adan said. *In your world it would translate into The Bridge City — the city where the Amato and Vesti have come together to forge a future for both races.*

Our home is close to here, Lyan growled impatiently, stepping onto a path of intricately entwined stones. *I want to spend our binding day in bed with our mate. There will be time for talk of history and philosophy later. Already I can hear someone approaching and we will be delayed. If we do not hurry, we risk not getting home at all.*

They'd taken only a few steps before a man rounded the corner and stopped in the middle of the pathway, blocking them.

Krista gasped in startled appreciation at the stranger. He was Amato, like Adan and Zeraac, but unlike Adan and his brother, the man in front of her had red-blond hair and wings interlaced with the same golden red. He made her think of an avenging angel she'd seen in a book as a child.

Both Lyan and Adan tensed when the stranger stepped close enough that Krista could feel the heat radiating off his body. Lyan growled and said, "What do you want, Draigon?"

The man's lip curled, but before he could say anything, Adan said, "This is not the way to forge peace between our peoples."

For several seconds longer, the man and Lyan glowered at each other until finally the man's gaze found Adan's and he nodded his head in acknowledgement. "I come to greet your new bond-mate and to tell her that soon her friend will join her on Belizair. The scientists have determined that the human female, Savannah, has the Fallon gene marker that matches mine."

Before Krista could reply, Lyan growled, "To harm one of the Vesti is to declare war on all of us, Draigon."

The stranger's eyes narrowed. "There will be no war. In true Vesti fashion, your cousin took what did not belong to him, but my mate would be dead if he had not been there to interfere. For that reason and that reason alone, I will accept him as a co-mate."

Without warning, Draigon leaned forward and pressed his lips to Krista's, then turned and strode past them, toward the portal.

Apprehension filled Krista as she watched him. The thought of him being with Savannah and Kye...

Do not worry, Adan said, *Draigon comes from an honorable house. He will do all that is in his power to make your friend happy. The future of his house and his heart depends on it.*

Epilogue

The sight of Adan's mate had almost distracted Draigon from the anger that Lyan's presence always inspired. By the stars, she had been exquisite.

Draigon had resigned himself to a human mate, though in truth he had never been drawn to any female other than those of his race, and the thought of a female with no wings...

Now he understood why some of the Fallon had been fascinated by them, why he had not seen any of the other human females brought back to form the Amato-Vesti bondings. Their mates had yet to let them out of bed!

Draigon's heart quickened and his cock stirred in anticipation of seeing what his own mate looked like. The Council scientist who had delivered the news of a match had said only that her hair was the deep red of a Sarien fire crystal and that she served as a law keeper on Earth.

A smile formed on Draigon's lips. It pleased him that she cared about law and order. The Amato had always been moved by such principals, though he had no intention of allowing her to continue such work after they were bonded.

His cock grew harder in anticipation. Where before he had been resigned, almost hoping that one of his brothers would be matched first, now he was anxious to get to the task of securing his mate and bringing her home, breeding her so that his line would continue.

He frowned. There had been no time to prepare a place, though a home would be made available in Winseka when they returned. Initially all Amato-Vesti bonded-mates had to settle in the bridge city so that their females would have a chance to be among other humans and so that the scientists could monitor them. Only after the birth of the first children were they allowed to live elsewhere on Belizair.

The frown grew deeper as his thoughts moved to Kye d'Vesti. He did not know much of Lyan's cousin, though there were some on the Council who claimed to like Kye, where all preferred to avoid Lyan, whose disdain and disrespect for Council rule raged before him like a sandstorm in the desert.

That Kye had taken Savannah, had already sunk both his mating teeth and his cock into her still sent a haze of anger through Draigon. By his very acts, Kye had already shown that he was like his cousin!

Only the fact that Draigon needed a Vesti co-mate and that Kye had both saved Savannah's life and called the scientist's attention to her so that she could be tested for the Fallon gene marker, enabled Draigon to move through the worst of his rage and accept the inevitable.

But by the stars, Savannah was his by Council decree and though he would share her, he would not do it willingly!

He entered the transport chamber, glad that he'd been granted permission to jump from the portal exit to where Kye and Savannah were, otherwise he would have been forced to endure endless Earth-hours using their primitive means of transportation.

Draigon grimaced. By all accounts, Earth was a backwater of a planet and he did not intend to remain there for long. He would secure his mate and return before the third sun rose and set on Belizair.

The stones in the chamber pulsed in a sequence of light and color and Draigon braced himself as the Ylan crystals in his wristbands pulled on the energy around them, preparing for the transmutation that preceded transport. The air in the chamber became charged and then before he could take a breath, he was on Earth.

He paused long enough to change into the clothing that the chambers were stocked with and then he used the Ylan crystals to both hide his wings and to transport him to Kye's location.

For a moment Draigon could only stare in amazed disbelief at the sight before him.

I would stand and greet you properly but as you can see, I am tied up right now, Kye said, his amused voice jerking Draigon's attention from the sight of a bound Vesti warrior lying on the ground to the human standing over him.

As if sensing his presence, Savannah turned toward Draigon then, and lust poured into him even as the breath was forced from his chest to be replaced by feelings such as he had never known. He moved forward, with only one thought, to claim his mate.

Enjoy an excerpt from:
ONLY HUMAN

Copyright © CHARLENE TEGLIA, 2007.
All Rights Reserved, Ellora's Cave Publishing, Inc.

Damon Thorne held the car keys she'd given him. The faint imprint of her personality, her presence, lay there in his hand, and he couldn't have stopped himself from closing his fist around it any more than he could have stopped the storm.

She was here.

If he had been a man given to emotional displays, he might have smiled. He might have shouted his triumph to the lightning-cut sky.

Instead, he merely closed his fist around the leather that belonged to her and walked with his usual measured strides to the car.

Her suitcase matched the key holder. Thorne noted that detail with a faint sense of tender amusement. She liked neatness and order. Liked things to match.

She also didn't like the dark. He'd begun to grow concerned when the skies darkened and she didn't arrive. He'd turned on the porch light for her and waited.

It seemed to Thorne that he had waited for her forever.

He wondered if she knew him, if she'd felt the shock of awareness and recognition he'd felt when he touched her. He hadn't been able to resist that, touching her, not when she was there in front of him and he could see her silk-covered, rain-dampened breasts, nipples tight and hard against the fabric. It had been all he could do not to cover them with his hands, stroking her nipples with his thumbs while the soft weight of her breasts filled his palms.

Desire. It raced through his blood, heated to the flash point by nothing more than the thought of her. Impatience followed. The woman he wanted was here, but he couldn't act on his desires just yet. He would be patient with her for the moment.

He would have to be. Because he was everything she feared most.

* * * * *

The power failed just as she finished rinsing her hair. Elaine opened her eyes to darkness, swore and groped for the knobs to turn off the shower.

The perfect ending to a perfect day, she thought. How hard would it be to find a towel in an unfamiliar place in total darkness?

She slid the shower curtain back and stepped out, taking care not to slip. Where was the towel bar? Elaine groped her way along the wall until her hands closed on fabric. Ah. There. She pulled the towel loose and wrapped it around herself.

A knock sounded on the bathroom door. "All right in there?"

"Yes," she answered. She tucked one end of the towel between her breasts, making a sort of sarong, felt water trickling down her neck from her wet hair and grimaced. Was there a second towel? She felt around and located a smaller towel, used it to blot most of the moisture from her hair and rehung it in the dark.

"I've got a flashlight for you here," her host said. "I'll set it next to the door."

"Thank you."

Elaine waited until she heard his footsteps moving away and then opened the door. The flashlight was easy to spot, right where he'd said it would be, and turned on. She picked it up and let out a long breath of relief. She had light. She wasn't dripping wet. She could find her way back to her room and get dressed without having to be rescued by a strange man while she wore nothing but a towel.

Would that be so bad? The unexpected thought was followed by an image so vivid it stopped Elaine in her tracks. The man, slowly untucking the towel's corner that held her makeshift cover in place, then unwrapping her and letting the towel fall at her feet. Leaving her naked. As she imagined that he stood in silence, looking at her, she felt her nipples pebbling into hard buds, her sex swelling with anticipation, growing hot and slick.

Elaine slammed the lid on her imagination and forced her feet to start moving again. Her body, however, remained aware and aroused, as if the man's presence had woken long-buried responses and needs.

Safely in the bedroom with the door shut behind her, Elaine leaned up against it, clutching her flashlight and debating what to do next. The fire provided soft, indirect illumination while casting shadows. The beam from her flashlight revealed her suitcase, sitting at the foot of the bed. The shirt he'd loaned her, which she'd left on the bed before going to take her shower, was gone. Presumably he was wearing it once again.

She should open the suitcase. Pull out some clothes. Put them on, arming herself against runaway fantasies and her body's traitorous rebellion in the process.

Elaine closed her eyes and imagined what she wanted to do instead. Take off the towel. Walk naked across the room and lay down on the bed. Touch herself the way she ached to be touched.

"Get a grip," she said out loud.

How embarrassing would that be if her host came to check on her and caught her masturbating?

Another imaginary picture unfolded in her mind. She sprawled naked on the bed, one hand pleasuring her breast, while the other moved between her legs. She explored the slick folds of her sex, stroked the sensitive bud of nerves at the top, then slid a finger into the tight opening below. The man watched her, his eyes fixed on hers and burning with hunger.

Jesus. She was losing her mind.

Or was it something worse? Was it starting again? Elaine made a small sound and slid down the door until she sat on the oak plank flooring. She'd buried her sex drive and her visions both, locked them away. If her long-denied sexual needs were breaking free, what if the rest broke loose, too?

"Damn you, Mickey," she whispered into the darkened room. If she were working at her usual pace, this wouldn't be happening. And she wouldn't be here, alone in a house with a man she was entirely too aware of, in the grip of something she might not be able to control.

Why an electronic book?

We live in the Information Age—an exciting time in the history of human civilization, in which technology rules supreme and continues to progress in leaps and bounds every minute of every day. For a multitude of reasons, more and more avid literary fans are opting to purchase e-books instead of paper books. The question from those not yet initiated into the world of electronic reading is simply: *Why?*

1. *Price.* An electronic title at Ellora's Cave Publishing and Cerridwen Press runs anywhere from 40% to 75% less than the cover price of the exact same title in paperback format. Why? Basic mathematics and cost. It is less expensive to publish an e-book (no paper and printing, no warehousing and shipping) than it is to publish a paperback, so the savings are passed along to the consumer.

2. *Space.* Running out of room in your house for your books? That is one worry you will never have with electronic books. For a low one-time cost, you can purchase a handheld device specifically designed for e-reading. Many e-readers have large, convenient screens for viewing. Better yet, hundreds of titles can be stored within your new library—on a single microchip. There are a variety of e-readers from different manufacturers. You can also read e-books on your PC or laptop computer. (Please note that Ellora's Cave does not endorse any specific brands.

You can check our websites at www.ellorascave.com or www.cerridwenpress.com for information we make available to new consumers.)

3. *Mobility.* Because your new e-library consists of only a microchip within a small, easily transportable e-reader, your entire cache of books can be taken with you wherever you go.

4. *Personal Viewing Preferences.* Are the words you are currently reading too small? Too large? Too... ANNOYING? Paperback books cannot be modified according to personal preferences, but e-books can.

5. *Instant Gratification.* Is it the middle of the night and all the bookstores near you are closed? Are you tired of waiting days, sometimes weeks, for bookstores to ship the novels you bought? Ellora's Cave Publishing sells instantaneous downloads twenty-four hours a day, seven days a week, every day of the year. Our webstore is never closed. Our e-book delivery system is 100% automated, meaning your order is filled as soon as you pay for it.

Those are a few of the top reasons why electronic books are replacing paperbacks for many avid readers.

As always, Ellora's Cave and Cerridwen Press welcome your questions and comments. We invite you to email us at Comments@ellorascave.com or write to us directly at Ellora's Cave Publishing Inc., 1056 Home Avenue, Akron, OH 44310-3502.

COMING TO A BOOKSTORE NEAR YOU!

ELLORA'S CAVE

Bestselling Authors Tour

Cerridwen, the Celtic Goddess of wisdom, was the muse who brought inspiration to storytellers and those in the creative arts. Cerridwen Press encompasses the best and most innovative stories in all genres of today's fiction. Visit our site and discover the newest titles by talented authors who still get inspired - much like the ancient storytellers did, once upon a time.

Discover for yourself why readers can't get enough
of the multiple award-winning publisher
Ellora's Cave.

Whether you prefer e-books or paperbacks,
be sure to visit EC on the web at
www.ellorascave.com

for an erotic reading experience that will leave you
breathless.